Sweet Deal Sealed

DONUT LADY COZY MYSTERY, BOOK 1

JUDITH A. BARRETT

WOBBLY CREEK, LLC

Sweet Deal Sealed

Donut Lady Cozy Mystery, Book 1

Published in the United States of America by Wobbly Creek, LLC

2020 Georgia

wobblycreek.com

Sweet Deal Sealed

Second Edition Copyright 2020 by Judith A. Barrett

First Edition Copyright 2018 by Judith A. Barrett

All Rights Reserved. No parts of this book may be reproduced, stored, or transmitted in any form or by any means, electronic, mechanical, photocopying, recording, or otherwise, without the prior written permission of the copyright owner, except for brief excerpts for reviews.

Sweet Deal Sealed, Second Edition is a work of fiction. Names, characters, businesses, places, events, locales, and incidents either are the products of the author's imagination or used in a fictitious manner. Any resemblance to actual persons, living or dead, or actual events is purely coincidental.

Cover by Wobbly Creek, LLC

Second Edition ebook: ISBN 978-1-733-12414-0

First Edition ebook: ISBN 978-1-732-29890-3

Second Edition Paperback: ISBN 978-1-7331241-5-7

Dedication

Sweet Deal Sealed is dedicated to donut shops, people who encourage children to read, and the color pink.

Chapter One

"The voices say we need to move." Shorty picked up her tray, and I followed her. Shorty was one of my few friends in the Ohio prison where I'd spent the past eleven years, eleven months, three weeks, and one day of my life. She was a dozen years younger than me, but we were staunch friends. We dropped off our breakfast trays and strolled toward the exit.

A woman two rows from us shouted and flung her tray at the inmate across the table from her. The edge of the tray caught the second woman across the bridge of her nose. Blood gushed down her shirt, and she collapsed to the floor. Someone slashed the first woman from her cheek to her ear, and a skirmish erupted at the farthest table from the exit. Shorty and I scooted out of the cafeteria. According to prison lore, whenever there's a fight, there's a murder.

"It'll be a rough 'un. Catch you later." Shorty scurried to the left, and I headed right. When I pushed open the prison library door, I paused and scanned the room. The welcoming fragrance of apples and cinnamon belied the cafeteria melee and stark surroundings beyond the library.

"Morning, Teach." The tall librarian had twisted her gray-streaked brown hair into a bun on top of her head, but unruly wisps escaped. She worked out in the gym every evening and was muscular from lifting weights and lean from running. "Nobody here except for me. It's either a good sign or a bad sign."

The labels on my clothing read *O'Brien, Karen* with my inmate number, but in my current world where everyone had a prison name, Teach worked for me.

Charlotte set a carton on the counter and brushed hair away from her face. "Here are the books you asked me to order, Karen. Are you sure about this? These are children's comic books, not adult paperbacks. I'm not sure I could have gotten these books approved if the captain had been in his office when I ordered them. Aren't you worried somebody will take offense and get the idea you don't think they're smart enough to read? Easy way to get a knife planted in your kidney."

I shrugged. "Isn't that a possibility every day? I discovered in my years of teaching children that a graphic novel was less intimidating for a reluctant reader with a short attention span than a book with pages full of words. Research shows adult learners are just as receptive because of the depth of the storyline and characters in graphic novels. We'll see, won't we?"

"I'm sure you're right. I admit I had my doubts about the advisability of teaching inmates to read when I first came here, but you've turned me into a believer. The desire to learn and the level of confidence that literacy has brought to this facility is amazing."

I reached into the opened box and stacked the books on the book cart. "I've cleared a shelf for the graphic novels and plan to showcase books on a table for curious readers."

As I loaded the books onto their new shelf, Shorty sauntered into the library. "Looks abandoned."

"You're here early, Shorty." Charlotte's peevish tone startled me. "You're not scheduled for library duty until this afternoon. You know my rules. Come back..."

"I wanted to get a peek at those newfangled books Teach ordered. She around?"

"Back shelf with the books," I called out.

"Shoulda known." Shorty chuckled as she headed my way. Shorty told me years ago that prison makes everybody crazy, but she was crazy before she came to prison. "The rest of them is amateurs," she cackled. Books were the basis of our friendship, at least in the beginning. Shorty was a voracious reader and an avid supporter of my efforts to teach women to read.

Shorty pulled an envelope out of the top of her shirt, set it on the cart, and handed me books as I put them in order. We wore the same gray uniforms, but because she was under four-foot ten inches tall, she rolled up her pants legs three times. I was a few inches taller and needed to turn up my pants legs only twice. Shorty didn't shower often, and her rank odor burned my eyes.

"You're extra ripe today, Shorty. You about due for a shower?"

"Somebody might try to sneak up on me. Like my old classmate, Ivy Gold. Her given name is Idella Violetta, but she is Poison Ivy. The voices say that's how I'm going to die. Crazy, right?"

"Maybe to the amateurs." I smiled.

Shorty snorted. "You remember everything, don't you, Teach? That's a talent. I see patterns. Patterns of death. Strange talent, but there I am."

"I heard rumblings about a grudge match today." Charlotte joined us.

Shorty flinched and dropped the book she held on top of the envelope. "Don't sneak up on folks, Charlotte. I'm not the only one who gets nervous when people show up sudden-like behind a person."

"Sorry, Shorty. You must be extra anxious because you're here off schedule."

I side-glanced at Charlotte then returned my attention to shelving books. *Strange comment. But who am I to judge strange?*

"You're the schedule person, Charlotte, not me, but if the staff's aware of more trouble, guess I better get to the kitchen. Don't want to get caught up in no mess," Shorty said.

After Shorty left, Charlotte said, "Sensible. Take a break for the rest of the day. I wouldn't mind locking up the library."

"I never turn down the offer of a break. Thanks."

I strolled past the door that led to the outside exercise area and stared out the window.

"What's up, Teach? Looking for somebody?" A guard asked.

"Thinking about fresh air and a little space."

The guard opened the door, and I stretched then headed to the track. When I first came to the prison twelve years ago at forty-seven, I jogged the track. I snorted. *Not anymore.*

When the warning horns blasted, the doors locked. I moved away from the doors but stayed near a wall where other women huddled in loose groups to avoid any fight that might break out in the common area. The potential of murder existed, but we counted on the rule of safety in numbers, the herd mentality. *A killer is less likely to single me out in this sea of gray.*

We held our collective breath until two blasts signaled the all-clear then we resumed our activities. After I finished my exercise circuit, I returned to the library and discovered Charlotte had not returned to unlock the doors.

Is she coming back? Should I wait for her?

Three women bustled past me. "Go home, Teach," a woman I knew from my hallway hissed, and I rushed to my cell as the loudspeakers announced lockdown.

The somber mood of the hallway spoke to the common belief of the inevitability of a murder. That evening, we were still in lockdown, and a guard rolled a cart with our meals to our cells. The guard avoided my gaze. His mouth was tight.

"What happened?" I asked.

"Sorry, Teach. Can't say," he whispered and pushed his cart to the next cell.

A woman toward the end of the hallway shouted. "Who was it? Tell me. Was it Ruby? Say it wasn't Ruby."

The hallway exploded in a guttural response of fear with the cacophony of women crying out names. I sat with my tray and pushed my corn into four neat squares then covered my plate. My shoulders tensed, and I shuddered. The shouts and screams turned to wails. "No, no," reverberated in the hallway.

I sat on my bed and covered my ears. As the lights dimmed then went out, the whimpers and moans replaced the shouts and loud cries, and I lay my head on my pillow. Screams and a familiar, rank odor woke me. Shorty stood by my bed.

"How did you get in here?" I whispered.

Shorty screamed, and I tried to shush her until I noticed the blood that soaked her shirt and dripped onto the floor. The bloody tip of a knife stuck out on the left side of her chest and pulsated with every heartbeat.

I gaped in horror. "You were stabbed in the back. The tip..." I covered my mouth to stifle my scream.

Shorty lost her balance and grabbed onto my bed to keep from falling. She spoke in such a soft voice that I leaned closer to hear her. "Never interrupt your enemy when she is making a mistake." She pushed away from my bed and screeched as she lurched through my cell bars to the hall. Shadows billowed into my cell, and I couldn't breathe.

I sat up and gasped for air as sweat rolled down my face and back. I wrapped my arms around my knees and rocked to stay awake.

Sobs from the hallway woke me early the next morning. I had fallen asleep against the wall with my knees bent and my feet flat on the bed. My neck, legs, and back ached, and I moaned as I stretched. My food tray from the night before was still in its slot. Voices from the hallway increased in volume as the rattle of the food cart announced breakfast. Shorty said not all the voices in the hallway were real, and she knew the difference. "You can do it, Teach. Just listen."

Maybe I will, Shorty.

A guard I didn't recognize removed my tray from the night before and slid in the breakfast tray. I uncovered my breakfast and found a small box of cereal, a carton of milk, and coffee. *No one cooking in the kitchen this morning.*

I cleaned up for the day at the tiny metal sink then sipped on the lukewarm coffee and munched on the dry cereal.

"Any news?" someone called out.

"Heard it was Shorty," someone else answered.

"I knew that," I mumbled. "She came to see me. So I'd know."

I pushed away my tray and rushed to the toilet where I lost my meager breakfast.

After the staff picked up our breakfast trays, two blasts of the all-clear horn sounded the end of lockdown, and our version of normal life resumed.

When I entered the library, Charlotte beamed. "Morning, Teach. Big event coming up, and we can start the thirty-day countdown. Do I have the dates right?"

"Hard to believe." *And hard to believe Shorty's dead.*

"I hear the last month is the longest, but you'll be fine. Three people signed up for reading lessons this morning, and the two who missed yesterday will be here too. Need any help with the books we got in yesterday?"

"No, I'm almost finished." I returned to my cart near the new books, and everything was as I'd left it.

Two women came into the library in a heated conversation.

"I'm turning this book in," one said as she dropped a book on the counter.

"So I can check it out," the other added.

"You know we have two additional copies of this book on the shelf," Charlotte said.

"I read faster than she does, and she gets mad when I get ahead of her," the first woman said. "She reads the book after I do, so it isn't a competition…"

"That way we can stay friends."

Someone dies, but we slip into our routines the next day. For sanity's sake?

When I picked up the book that was on the cart, I stared at Shorty's envelope and stacked the remaining books on top of it. After I shelved all but five of the books, I rolled the cart toward the library table I'd designated for graphic novels. On the way, I stopped at the reference section and selected a dictionary to add to the table then slipped the envelope into a thesaurus. I arranged four books and the dictionary in the middle of the table then returned the cart to the front with a graphic novel under my arm.

My new reader, Duchess, waited for me in the reading room. She sat with her back straight and her hands in her lap. *Always poised.*

"Good morning, Teach. I'm here for my first lesson. Have you selected a book for me? I think I might like historical fiction."

"I have a surprise for you. You are the first to read our new books."

She beamed. "It's only right. I should be the first."

I sat next to her and placed the graphic novel on the table. As Duchess opened the book and flipped through the pages, her eyes widened.

"This can't count as reading. It's got pictures."

"It's my reading secret. The pictures help you learn to read faster." I smiled with more confidence than I felt. *If Duchess buys into graphic novels, her followers will too.*

She gazed at my face. "Okay. You're the expert, and I want to learn to read. Let's do this, Teach."

At the end of our forty-five-minute session, I had read the first chapter to her, and she had struggled through the first three pages with help. Duchess dabbed at the beads of sweat on her forehead and patted her neck with a ripped piece of cloth she called her *handkerchief.*

"That was intense," she said. "Same time tomorrow?"

"Same time tomorrow." My slow nod was solemn even though I was singing a song of triumph in my heart. I glanced up and squinted at the shadows dancing in the corner. *Shorty heard voices, and I have nightmares and see shadows?*

Duchess paused and gazed at me before she opened the door. "Shorty was my friend. She told me last week the voices said I could trust you."

I bit my lip. *Shorty tried to prepare her friends.*

At the end of the day, I stopped by Charlotte's desk with the thesaurus. "Check this out for me?"

"I've already turned off the computer. Nobody else has even touched that book in the three years I've been here. Take it." Charlotte waved as I headed to the door. "See you in the morning."

"Have a good night." I carried the thesaurus to my cell. I sorted through the Christmas cards I had received from my former home insurance company and slipped Shorty's envelope in with my meager stack of mail. I added the thesaurus to the four other books on my shelf.

The next morning, I read each Christmas card and examined the inserted advertisement sheets. When I opened Shorty's envelope, I found a page with addresses and dates marked *from* and *to* for each address. The first date was twenty-five years ago, and the latest date was three years ago. The most amount of time between the start and end dates for any one address was five years. *Places where Shorty lived?* I copied the information inside three of my Christmas cards and returned the envelope to the thesaurus.

After breakfast, a guard asked, "What's the first thing you'll do when you get out, Teach?"

"Move to my hometown in Georgia where it's warm."

He chuckled. "Smartest thing I've ever heard."

When I reached the library, Duchess waited in the reading room. Her face was flushed, and she fanned herself with a pamphlet.

"I am agitated today, Teach, but I will strive to focus on reading. My handkerchief is missing." She pulled a piece of cloth out of the top of her shirt. "Twitch gave it to me. It's threadbare but soft. She found a ripped sheet in the laundry and fashioned a new hanky for me." She waved it and smiled. "The stray threads remind me of lace when I flutter it."

I returned her smile. "I like the delicate look it has."

I sat next to her and opened our book to the first page. "Let's see how far you get then I'll read the second chapter."

Before we started, Charlotte tapped on the door jamb. "May I speak to you for a moment in my office, Teach?"

After she closed her office door, she sat at her desk and drummed her fingers on her calendar pad as she glanced at her computer. "Is everything okay? Are you safe? Duchess seemed anxious today, and I was worried you might be in danger."

"She's fine." I gazed at her face. "Are you doing okay?"

She rose and leaned against her desk, and her eyes narrowed. "Why wouldn't I be? What do you know?"

"Haven't you noticed the tension in the air?"

"You're right, Teach. There are several unpredictable, violent inmates that make me nervous, and Duchess is at the top of that list. Just be careful."

I reached for the doorknob and paused. "Have you had a problem with her?"

"Only once, and I reported her immediately; three days in her cell settled her down. I monitor her because I never know when she might retaliate."

Charlotte shifted away from her desk and assumed a relaxed stance. "Shorty's voices said I was in danger. If they hadn't forewarned me, it might have been much worse."

"I'll remember that. Thanks."

I returned to the reading room. "Sorry about the interruption. Ready to read?"

After Duchess finished the sixth page, she beamed and patted her face with her new handkerchief. "The pictures are an excellent memory-jogger for the written word. You are a brilliant educator."

"I know it's hard work for you, but your progress is amazing." I turned the pages to chapter two but paused. "Your vocabulary is excellent. I can't help but wonder why you never learned to read, but I don't mean to pry."

"My story is not unique. I can never remember a time that my mother was not ill or injured. She had her fourth child, my baby brother, when I was seven. My father left before the baby was born, and I was glad. He was a leech and a brute. I never attended school because I supported the family with three paper routes. Mother told me to listen to educated people and emulate their language.

She died when I was nine, and I talked my way into a housekeeping job at a fancy hotel to support my siblings."

I raised my eyebrows. "Nine?"

She smiled. "I was always big for my age and spoke with confidence."

"I can imagine. What an insightful gift your mother gave you."

At the end of chapter two, Duchess rose. "Thank you, Teach. I'll read chapter one to you tomorrow. One more thing. Shorty's voices said it's important to know where a person comes from. I reminded her only short-timers talked about the outside. She nodded and said she was from Tennessee. I'm from West Virginia."

"I'm from Georgia."

Duchess nodded. "Thank you. It's been a pleasure to have made your acquaintance."

After my last morning reader left, Twitch met me at the library door on my way to lunch.

"Ain't quite ready to learn to read them words, Teach," she said. "I brung you a sandwich. Would you read to me?"

I turned back to the reading room, and Twitch followed me. "What kind of story would you like?"

"I'd like a story from one of them pitcher books Duchess tole me about. Can we sit on the floor? Me and Mama sat on the floor when she read me a story. She always said someday I could learn to read too."

"She was right. We can sit on the floor if you'll help me back up."

Twitch chuckled. "That's what Mama always said."

Twitch sat on the floor. "Criss-cross, applesauce," she said in a sing-song voice.

"Ring-around-the-rosie, all-fall-down for me." I held onto the table as I lowered myself to the floor.

Twitch giggled.

After I settled into a position with the least amount of pain, I opened the book and pointed to each word as I read. I glanced at Twitch while she focused on the words. At the end of the first page, Twitch said, "Read it again so I can read with you. That's what Mama did, and I learned some words."

I pointed and read the first word, and Twitch parroted me. After we read the first page, I asked, "Ready for the next page?"

"Yes."

After an hour, we were on page ten. "You are picking up lots of words, Twitch. Well done."

"Shorty told me I needed to learn to read. She said that every day. I miss Shorty."

"I do too. She was a good friend."

"She told me her voices wanted me to know falling was dangerous. She said the voices only cared about her friends. I'm glad I was Shorty's friend. I'm careful on the stairs." She pursed her lips. "I'll be back again. Maybe tomorrow or next week." Twitch hopped up then helped me to my feet.

I groaned as I struggled up. "Thanks, Twitch. Someone wise said the best exercise is to get on the floor and back up again three times a day. That's one for me."

Twitch giggled. "Want me to hang around? I could help you up two more times."

"We could do that, but I'd need a nap first." I chuckled.

The sound of footsteps approached the reading room, and Twitch's face paled.

"I was worried when you weren't at lunch, Teach." Charlotte stood in the doorway with her arms crossed. "You need to manage your time better."

She strode away, and Twitch peeked out from the doorway. "She's in her office. I can get away now." Twitch dashed out of the library.

No love lost there on either side. I ate the ham and cheese sandwich Twitch had brought me.

Bribes work. I'm on Twitch's side. I snickered.

After I straightened up the reading room, I found a guard and asked if I could speak with a supervisor.

"Complaint about me? Because if it is, I'm a supervisor," she winked.

"Are you in training for customer service?" I smiled. "I have an idea, but everything goes through channels."

"Isn't that the truth? I'll get the process started for you."

———ele———

Two days later, a guard stopped by before I left my cell on my way to breakfast. "Ready for a meeting?"

I grabbed a list I'd prepared, and he led the way to the captain's office.

"Come on in, Teach. Whatcha got?" Captain Littlefield waved at a chair. "Have a seat." The guard left and closed the door.

The captain's gray hair had remnants of dark-brown, and he wore dark-framed bifocals and a white long-sleeved uniform shirt with a captain's badge on his pocket. His chair creaked when he moved, and his desk was gray government-issued metal and littered with framed snapshots of families with children and the captain with a woman whose smile lit up the no-frills office. A formal photo on the wall over the metal file cabinet was of a dark-haired, thinner captain in dress uniform.

"I'm scheduled to be released in less than a month and have a proposal to continue the reading program. I'd like to recommend five women to continue teaching others to read. They are patient, mature, and have demonstrated a talent with dealing with the younger, angry women in particular that make up the largest population of nonreaders." I handed him a sheet of paper with five names.

"Good choices. You didn't list Charlotte. Any reason?"

"Charlotte manages the library. She's available if any of the tutors have a problem with a student and can serve as an advisor for the new reading teachers."

"Makes sense. What's your plan?"

"I'd like to get together with the new teachers as a group for three days for train-the-trainer sessions. Then they can work with readers on their own, and I'll be available in the library for consultation. We'll have regular meetings as a group to discuss progress and answer questions."

"I'll get back to you by tomorrow with official approval. Meanwhile, you can approach your new teachers and schedule a meeting. Is it okay if I sit in on your first meeting?"

"I think word would get out, and nobody would show. Too much brass. Give us a guard we know and trust to represent you."

"McMillan?"

"Perfect. I plan to meet with the group at two o'clock today in the library."

He reached into his desk and handed me a business card. "This is my cell. You probably will never need it but consider it a link to an old friend."

The guard accompanied me back to my hallway. "Good luck, Teach." He saluted and sauntered down the hall.

I hurried to breakfast and made it in time to talk to each of the five women and invite them to meet at two. When I arrived at the library, Charlotte was in the history section.

"I have a plan to develop new reading tutors," I said. "Can we talk in your office?"

After I explained my plan, Charlotte asked, "Do you mind if I sit in on your meeting and training sessions? I could help as a mentor, and I'd like to write an article to share your process with librarians at other institutions."

"I'd love for the program to have formal documentation of the process, and others may have a program in place and could share best practices. I need to prepare a handout for today's meeting. Is there a computer and printer I could use?"

"The only computer connected to a printer is mine. You could use it if you don't mind me in the office while you're working. I have reports I need to complete by the end of the day, and I've procrastinated as long as I dare. I could pull the data together while you work then enter my final when you're done."

"Won't take me long, thanks."

I composed the first page of my handout while Charlotte sat next to me at her desk. I typed, and she shuffled and flipped through papers. I bumped her with my elbow as I typed because she was sitting so close.

"You have enough room?" I asked.

"I'm fine. Thanks," she said.

I'm not. I completed the second page, proofread my document then asked, "Can I save my document before I print?"

"Sure. Let me set you up a folder." She leaned on me, and I cringed from the invasion of my personal space. Charlotte took over the keyboard and created a folder on the desk. "Here you go. Easy to find."

I saved and printed copies of the document then left her office.

Two weeks earlier, I had designated a table near the reading room as my "office" and placed fourteen books on the table. I read a book every day then returned it to its shelf. I discovered not even Charlotte interrupted me while I read at my office table, *my magic privacy bubble. Or if she does, I don't hear her.*

On my way to the reading room, I picked up my day's book and shook off my peevishness. Once inside, I relaxed at the table and jotted notes on my copy of the handout then read.

At one thirty, Duchess glided into the reading room. "I don't mean to disturb you, Teach, but I understand you have a meeting at two with five potential candidates to serve as reading tutors. First, it's a most admirable endeavor. I applaud your dedication to keeping the program alive. Second, I desire to continue our lesson after your conference. What time shall I return?"

"I expect the meeting to last forty-five minutes to an hour at most."

"I shall return at three-ten. Thank you."

———*ele*———

At ten minutes until two, doubt washed over me, and my stomach churned. *Will it work? What if the tutors all quit? Or don't even show up? Will women continue to learn to read?*

"It's a good plan." I took in a good breath through my nose and pursed my lips to exhale as slowly as I could.

McMillan sauntered into the room two minutes early. He was one of the new guards, a recent graduate of the University of Cincinnati criminal justice program. His serious medium-brown caramel face broke into dimples when he smiled.

"Where do you want me to sit?" His soft Alabama drawl reminded me of home.

I counted the chairs. "Didn't think about seating. We need two more chairs. One for you and one for Charlotte."

"I'll grab them," he said. When he returned, we set the chairs together against the far wall, and Charlotte and the five prospective tutors spilled into the room.

After everyone selected a seat, I passed around the document.

"If you have questions as we go along, please ask. I won't answer questions; instead, I expect you to discuss the question and come up with your own answers."

"Teach is getting lazy," a woman said, and we laughed. After a half hour, we had covered the first page and moved on to the second. The discussion was animated and productive, and the five individuals moved forward in the bonding process of a support group. McMillan gave me a thumbs up and excused himself before we ended.

The women established a schedule for each one to provide tutoring sessions, and we agreed to meet the next two days at the same time for the trainer sessions.

After the group left, Charlotte said, "That went very well."

"I agree." I returned the two extra chairs to the library then recorded my thoughts for the next two sessions.

At three-ten, Duchess sashayed into the reading room. Charlotte hovered outside the room.

"Ready for my fool-hardy self-challenge?" Duchess asked.

"I'm ready, but it isn't fool-hardy. I know you'll do it. Give me a minute. I think Charlotte wants to talk to me."

I stepped outside the room and closed the door. "Is there something wrong? You're hovering. Do you have something to discuss that can't wait?"

"I was trying to guard you. The voices said I needed to stay close to you so you don't get hurt. Leave the door open, and I'll sit right outside."

I shook my head. "Now you're making me nervous. Go to your office. I'll be fine."

When she reached for a chair to scoot to the door, I raised my eyebrows. "If you're that worried, I'll get McMillan and ask him to sit in with us."

She slammed the chair into the table. "That's unnecessary."

After she stomped to her office, I returned to the reading room.

"Sorry. I owe you five extra minutes."

Duchess struggled through the first chapter. When a word frustrated her, and she couldn't figure it out, she'd say "cantaloupe," and we'd giggle. I wrote the words she missed, and when she ended chapter one, she had a vocabulary list. We reviewed her list then I read chapter two.

"Thank you, Teach. This is very hard work. Almost harder than anything I've ever done before." She chuckled. "I consider hearing the next chapter my reward. Will you assign me a tutor? How will that work?"

"We haven't decided yet. That's on the agenda for tomorrow. What would you suggest?"

"Whatever you do, there needs to be an understanding that if the reader and tutor combination isn't working, there is no shame in changing. Put your smart team to work on that."

"I like it. Thanks."

"Folklore dictates it is bad luck to mention how many days are left before a person's release; however, I rejoice in your reading progress." Duchess gazed at me. "I will miss you, Teach. You've been an inspiration to me."

We strolled out of the reading room and past the library desk. "Your support made a difference. Thank you and good catch on my books. Only wish I'd thought of it earlier."

Duchess paused before she reached the door. "You've been far more patient than I would have been."

As she left the library, I stared after her. *Why did Charlotte want me to think Duchess was dangerous?*

The next morning, I awoke before dawn. *One more day, Lord. Keep me out of trouble.* I washed my face and made up my bed. As the lights came on, the voices of women waking to yet another day in prison drifted down the hallway, and shadows skimmed the floor outside my cell and whispered, "Murdersss." I glared at the shadows, and they dissipated.

When I returned to the library with the thesaurus after lunch, Charlotte waited for me at my personal office table. Her eyes twinkled with excitement. "Tomorrow's your big release day. Are you thrilled?"

I returned the book to the reference shelf and joined Charlotte. "You know it's bad luck to mention a release day."

She dismissed my comment with a wave of her hand. "That's a silly superstition, but you're right. I'm sorry." She cleared her throat. "Did you hear the news?"

I narrowed my eyes. *This can't be good.*

"The captain charged Duchess with Shorty's murder this morning. Gossip says it was drugs or a love triangle. What do you think?"

"I think it's a mistake." I picked up my last book.

"Not surprised. Duchess was your special pet reader, wasn't she?" Charlotte flounced to her office.

I opened my book to read, but I seethed instead.

McMillan opened the door to the library. "Need to chat with you, Teach."

So much for my magic privacy bubble. I snorted.

He led the way but stopped after we passed the door to the exercise yard. "This is unofficial. It'll break later, but a guard found a handkerchief with blood on it hidden near the murder scene yesterday."

"Handkerchief? Duchess had her handkerchief after Shorty was killed. Duchess would never have allowed blood on her handkerchief. Not her style. Someone must have stolen it."

"We heard that too. Everything's preliminary." He strode away while I stared at his back. *Never had a guard trust me before.*

That evening, the whispers in the cafeteria buzzed with the news Duchess had been arrested for Shorty's murder and moved to a different prison. *Framed* was the consensus. Twitch threw her plate onto the floor, covered her ears with her hands, and screeched. A guard hurried to her and spoke in a soft voice as he guided her out of the cafeteria.

At lights-out, I lay on my bed and stared at the dark. My eyelids drooped.

I blinked. The dim light of a lantern hung in the corner of my cell. I tilted my head at the sound of the soft lapping of waves that licked against my bed. When I rolled to peer under my bed, water splashed onto my face. My bed floated on the lake in my cell.

My heart pounded. *Where are my oars? Who took my oars?*

My cell walls slid away and transformed into a narrow canyon with steep sides. The only light was a glimmer high above my head. The lake emptied into a rushing river, and my bed lurched against the rocks as it careened down the rapids. Faceless figures perched on the rocks and reached out to me as I sped past them. I grabbed the hand of a small figure and pulled it to my raft, but I lost my grip. I dived into the icy water to save the drowning creature, but I sank to the bottom where the small figure waited for me.

"Are we dead?" I asked.

"Only if we don't live," the creature said then it died, and the body drifted away.

I screamed and tried to swim after it, but I woke on the floor of my cell. I sobbed for the small figure that drowned. *I should have held on tighter.*

After my tears subsided, I leaned against my bed and stretched out my legs on the frigid concrete floor. Shadows slid into my cell, and when I waved them away, they hovered in a corner.

I'll wait here for morning.

At eleven o'clock, I sat in a straight-back chair with my hands folded in my lap while the warden processed my release from prison. He tapped his pen on the last page. "You're a nice lady, O'Brien. Find something nice to do. You have a plan?"

"Yes, sir. I do."

"I tell everyone not to look back. Nobody listens." He chuckled as he signed the last page. He rose and shook my hand. "I know I won't see you again."

"No, sir, you won't."

I had my savings, my retirement check, and the proceeds from the sale of my house. I planned to start fresh in my hometown in southern Georgia, far from where I met, married, and, according to my court conviction, murdered my cheating husband, Terry.

I carried my few possessions out to where a cab waited for me. *Don't look back.*

The faded blue taxicab with rusted fenders pulled up to a modest motel an hour from the Ohio prison where I'd lived for the past twelve years. The gray-haired cabbie jumped out with more energy than I expected for his age and weight, opened my door, and grabbed my suitcase out of the trunk. I gave him the prison voucher and a tip.

"Thanks, kid. Good luck to ya." He gave a quick salute and hopped into his old vehicle.

Long time since anybody's called me kid.

When I opened the lobby door, the sweet aroma of the vanilla candle at the desk wrapped around me. The pale green overstuffed visitors' chairs and the ink and watercolor drawings of boats and the ocean added to the atmosphere of serenity.

A young clerk with untamable curly dark hair pulled into a bun stood at the registration desk. She wore a crisp white shirt with the motel logo on the pocket. Her eyes crinkled with her smile. "Ms. O'Brien? Just need your signature."

After she completed my registration and handed me a key, she pointed to the hallway. "Turn right for your room, ma'am, and left for the business center."

I glanced over my shoulder to see who was behind me. *It's been a long time since anyone called me ma'am.*

When I opened my room door, I gasped. *Somebody made a mistake; this room's the luxury suite.* My room was three times the size of my cell and featured a double bed with a white comforter and a bathroom with a door that closed. I caught a whiff of lavender. *Duchess would love this.*

I pressed my hands against the mattress and marveled as my handprints slowly disappeared. The cream background and pink and yellow flowers of the overstuffed chair near the window gave the room an inviting, homey look. I rubbed my fingertips over the scarred wooden desk. *I love the patina and the feel of old wood.* I put my hands on my hips and surveyed the room. *No dirt, no stains. Everything's clean.*

I picked up the remote and sat on the flowered chair then slid the faux-leather footstool closer for my feet. After I turned on the television and changed channels, I lifted my chin and surveyed the room. "Any complaints?" No one answered.

With a flourish and a flick of my wrist, I turned off the television. No groans or shouts. *I am the ruler of the controller.*

When I peeked into the bathroom, my hand flew to my mouth at the sight of the white, fluffy bath towels, extra toilet paper, and full tissue box. *I had forgotten what it was like on the outside.* By contrast, my six-by-eight-foot cell had a metal sink, a toilet with no privacy, a threadbare once-white towel, and the pervasive odor of disinfectant.

The signs in the hallway pointed to the motel's business center. The empty room had a computer and paper for the printer. *When's the last time I used a computer and a printer?* I snickered. *Without a certain librarian making sure I didn't snoop through her files, that is.*

Chapter Two

I scooted the office chair up to the computer desk and searched the internet for a real estate agent in my hometown, Asbury, Georgia. I didn't recognize any of the names until a familiar one popped up at the end of the list. I cringed. *Shirley Warren was a real pain when we were kids.* I dialed the number on the listing. *Maybe she's mellowed.*

"Shirley? It's Karen O'Brien. Remember me? I'd like to buy a house in Asbury. Are you still an agent?"

"Karen? Karen O'Brien? We heard you went to prison in Ohio or Wisconsin. Are you on the lam? Are you sure you want to move back here, Karen? Nobody comes here on purpose. Do you know what you want? I have the perfect house for you. You can walk to town. You can still walk, right? You wouldn't believe how many people have had knee or hip replacements. Younger than us. In fact…"

"Shirley," I broke in. "Can we look at houses this week?" *Nope, hasn't mellowed a bit.*

We settled on a day, and I hurried back to my room. I closed the bathroom door, stripped, turned the shower faucet all the way to the left at full blast and watched the spray steam up the room. I stepped into the tub and hopped out. "Whew. Hot."

I turned down the water temperature, climbed back into the shower, and lathered up with the lavender and vanilla soap. I smiled. *There's not even a whiff of disinfectant.* I poured creamy shampoo over my wet hair, and the foamy suds filled the bathroom with the aroma of coconuts. After I rinsed, I grabbed the oversized towel and scrubbed myself dry. I had looked forward to shedding the institutional smell but hadn't imagined how powerful the impact of a lavender and vanilla fragrance would have on my spirit. *I could go for a walk outside if I felt like it.*

After I dressed, I grabbed my things and headed to the lobby. The young clerk's eyes widened. "Is everything okay, Ms. O'Brien? Are you checking out?"

I glanced down at my hands that carried my old suitcase and overflowing plastic bag. *I picked up everything.* My face warmed, and my ears burned.

"Please excuse me. I was worried something was wrong. I'll make sure no one bothers your room while you're out." The kindness and concern in her voice was a stark contrast to my animal instinct to keep my meager things close.

I cleared my throat. "Thank you. My room is wonderful. I won't be long."

I stepped outside, but my original excitement vanished. I trudged half a block then turned back. After I returned, I climbed into bed and cried over my brokenness. *I don't belong on the outside.*

I woke early the next morning while it was still dark. I showered in the hot water with the lavish lavender and vanilla. After I dressed, I opened the curtains and shifted the chair to gaze out the window while I waited for the sun to rise.

When the housekeeper tapped on my door and called out "Housekeeping," I jumped, and my heart pounded. I left the chain intact and peeked out.

The woman smiled, and I stepped into the hallway, stood outside the door while sweat rolled down my back, and waited for her to leave. *The only time staff entered a cell was for an unannounced search.* I looked at the floor and bit my lip. *Did I put the pen back on the counter after I signed in at the registration desk?*

The housekeeper came out with a damp towel in her hand. I glanced at her, and she nodded as she rolled the cart to the next room. "Give it a week. You'll be okay."

I expected to find my mattress tossed and my clothes dumped on the floor, but she had made my bed, replaced my damp towel, and left four bars of lavender and vanilla soap. I slumped down on the soft chair in relief. *I'll be okay in a week.*

I left my things and headed to the lobby. I paused before I turned the corner and inhaled then exhaled. I glanced back at my door. *Everything will be okay.*

An older clerk breezed past me from the other hallway. "Coffee's fresh," she said. I followed her to the lobby, and she pointed to a small room across from the desk. "Coffee, juice, and a light breakfast. Comes with your room. Help yourself."

I poured a cup of coffee and moved away to face the doorway with my back against the wall. When the pounding of my heart slowed, I cruised the breakfast buffet and picked out a container of yogurt. I refilled my coffee and sat at the table near my corner to eat my breakfast.

On my way to my room, I stopped at the desk. "Is there transportation to the bus station?" I asked.

The clerk smiled. "Our shuttle can take you there. It leaves in thirty minutes."

I'll be okay in a week.

The smell of unwashed bodies and diesel filled the bus depot. *Some things never change.* I settled into the molded plastic seat to wait for the station master to announce the boarding for my nineteen-hour bus ride to Albany, Georgia. I hugged my purse and plastic bag to my chest and held my suitcase tight between my knees.

"Albany, Georgia." The recorded announcement conveyed the same bored attitude the ticket clerk displayed when I bought my ticket. I shuffled onto the bus and slid into a window seat four rows from the front. The deodorized air irritated my throat, and I coughed. A woman with her hair in a tight bun frowned and scooted past me. An overweight man dropped into the seat next to me, and I bounced. I pulled the paperback I'd bought for the trip out of my purse and stuck my purse between me and the wall.

After our first stop, I glanced at the driver, and the shadows hid him. I gasped, and my seatmate peered at me. *What are the shadows doing here? I thought I'd left them in my cell.*

I crossed my arms, leaned against the window, and closed my eyes. The bus braked hard, and my head jerked. My eyes widened at the sixteen-wheeler that was inches from my window. The early morning haze hid the sky.

My seatmate leaned toward me and chuckled. "You slept right through our second stop at midnight, lady. Didn't miss nothing."

My eyes watered, and I blinked. *I'll bet my breath smells as foul as his.*

When the bus rolled into the Albany station, passengers jumped up to stand in the aisle. After everyone cleared the aisles, my seatmate pulled himself up using the seat in front of him as leverage and lumbered off the bus, and I followed him.

While I waited for the driver to unload my luggage, a woman in a red cardigan over a white blouse tapped my shoulder.

"Karen?" She peered at my face. She outweighed me by thirty pounds and was four inches taller. Her short, curly, blonde hair had streaks of highlights, and her makeup was impeccable. Even when we were kids,

Shirley was fastidious about her appearance and always wore a red jacket or sweater.

I nodded. "Shirley."

"You haven't changed a bit," she said. "Well, that's not exactly true. Where'd you get all the gray hair? Nobody I know has gray hair except the twenty-year-olds who are going for the gray look. I don't understand why. You'd think they'd prefer purple or red. Your bus was only forty-five minutes late. The station master told me that's not bad at all. It's about an hour's drive to Asbury. We'll get there about lunchtime then I've got houses for you to look at. There's one I think you'll like a lot, but I won't tell you which one. You can make up your own mind. Is that your suitcase?" Shirley pointed to my scuffed gray suitcase, which was the lone piece next to the bus.

I claimed my luggage, and Shirley led the way to her car. "I think the last time I rode on a bus was twenty years ago. They weren't much back then. Was your bus comfortable? Did you ride all night? I don't think I could sleep on a bus. Could you put up your feet? Here's my car."

"You still talk as much as you ever did, Shirley."

"Really? I found a nice room for you and reserved it for a month, but I got a call this morning. The room isn't available after all. Some people are narrow-minded. I finally found a motel kind of close in with a microwave and small refrigerator that will take you. I have two vacant houses for sale you can see, and the owners will go with a short-term lease until your house deal closes. Nobody else was interested in...well..."

Shirley frowned and cleared her throat.

So much for thinking I could have a fresh start.

"You okay with a quick lunch? We can grab a sandwich at Gus's shop. You remember Gus's, right? Maybe you remember when it was Willie's. Gus was three years behind us in school. He bought out Willie when Willie retired. Still good sandwiches. It's about an hour from here to Asbury, but you probably remember that."

I stared at the passing green countryside then leaned back and closed my eyes. The drone of the car tires on the road and Shirley's voice must have put me out because when Shirley slowed, I opened my eyes. *Asbury.*

"Here we are. Gus's shop. You napped on the way. I'll bet you didn't sleep very well on that bus. I wouldn't have."

When we stepped inside, I inhaled the aroma of the freshly baked bread and memories swirled in my head. I stared at the wooden floor and stained vinyl countertop, and smiled. *The sandwich shop hasn't changed since I was in high school, and Mama and I'd have lunch together once a month.* I scanned the menu on the wall for my favorite.

The tall young man behind the counter asked, "Ready to order?"

"Turkey and cranberry sandwich on wheat bread and sweet tea." *Mama and I would split a sandwich.*

"My usual," Shirley said. "We'll take them to go."

We took our lunches to the town park across the street from Gus's. I bit into my turkey sandwich and closed my eyes. *Just like I remembered.* The mockingbirds and cardinals serenaded us while we ate. *I want to spend the rest of my life eating lunch outside.*

After we returned to Shirley's car, her phone rang. She pulled a sheet out of the middle of a file folder on her console and handed it to me. She propped her phone against her shoulder, took notes with one hand, and twirled her hair with the other.

Shirley ended her call. "We'll go to the one I like best first. If you like it, we won't go to the other. It's the perfect house for you. A 1920s-era, two-bedroom bungalow with a spacious front porch, and it's within walking distance of downtown. The owner moved to Alaska and is eager to lease or sell it, so you can move in right away. Will you need to buy furniture, or do you have yours in storage?"

"I have my favorite furniture in storage, but I'll need a bed."

"Then you could move in while you wait for your furniture, right?" After the third turn, Shirley pulled to the curb. "We're here. Did you look over the listing? It includes a washer and dryer. That's a money-saving bonus. Isn't this yard nice? Not a lot of maintenance. A little mowing, but there's a lawn care business that takes care of most of the houses in the neighborhood. Lawn service is very convenient for a single person. Nice big trees. Shade's a premium in southern Georgia."

When Shirley opened the front door, I fell in love with the wooden floors, the distinctive farmhouse window trim, the kitchen and pantry, and the simple layout of the cottage-style home.

"You're right, Shirley. You've found the perfect house for me. It's cozy, and I love the convenience of walking to town." *After twelve years in a cramped cell, the bungalow is a palace.*

"I knew it. I have the paperwork ready for you. Ready to shop for a bed? The furniture store will deliver. You'll need some linens and kitchen things too. We can shop this afternoon. I have the papers right here. You'll just need to sign them then I'll call the owner. Do you want to go shopping or are you too exhausted after your bus trip? I'll take you to the motel if you like after we finish our paperwork then pick you up in the morning at eight or nine. The original motel owners retired. I don't know the new owner, but the old owners served breakfast. Would that work for you?"

"Shopping tomorrow sounds good." *Not to mention giving my ears a rest.*

After I signed the paperwork, we headed to the motel.

"The motel's not new, but it's nice. I called in your reservation earlier, but no one answered. They must be busy. I left a message though, so you are all set." The motel was three miles outside of town. Shirley parked at the motel entrance then waved after I rolled my suitcase to the entrance. The parking lot was empty.

Must be early for check in.

When I opened the door, the musty odor and the frayed, stained carpeting in the empty lobby was a sharp contrast to my previous motel. I tapped the tarnished desk bell on the counter. The click of the battery-operated clock on the wall behind the desk ticked off the minutes as I waited.

After five minutes, I tapped the bell a second time. When another five minutes passed, I rolled my suitcase to the door.

"You in a big hurry or something?" A scratchy voice behind me broke the silence.

When I turned, the emaciated woman with a cigarette in her hand scowled. "I suppose you're that jailbird I heard so much about. I have one room left. I take only cash, and you also owe me a two-hundred-dollar security deposit. Not refundable. Cash. I count the towels, so don't even think about stealing anything."

I continued to the door.

"Hey. You can't leave. I saved this room for you. You owe me fifty dollars for holding a room. Cash."

Shadows rushed in from the front door and darkened the lobby, and I snickered as I strode away from the motel.

"Thank you, shadows."

I rolled my suitcase on the bumpy shoulder as I hiked to Asbury. I was nervous about being on foot on the shoulder of the highway, but no traffic passed me either way. After twenty minutes, I stared at the sign, *Asbury 2 miles*, and froze. *Was I too rash? Did I let pride get the best of me? What's my plan? Where am I going to stay tonight?*

I trudged on. *I've got options.* I smiled at the fields of cotton and peanuts and the beauty of the rows of old pecan trees in their orderly orchards.

I snorted. *I just don't know what they are off-hand.*

Thirty-five minutes later, an old single-story motel with rooms that opened to the parking lot was on my right. The letters *o* and *t* on the neon sign, *Asbury Motel*, were burned out, and the gutters across the front of the building drooped. There were three cars and a truck parked in front of rooms. *More guests here than at that other one.*

When I entered the office, a woman who was the same size and age as Shorty rushed from behind the desk to greet me. "You poor thing. Did you get dropped off on the highway? You're better off. Do you need a room for the night, or do you want to call someone to come get you? Let me get you some coffee."

She hurried back with a hot cup of coffee. "Do you take cream or sugar?"

I accepted the cup she offered and fought off the tears from her kindness. "No, thank you. This is great. I need a room for the night, and I need to call a friend this evening."

"I'll put you in the room closest to the office in case you need anything. We have old phones in the rooms, but they work. Our walls are paper thin, so if you knock on your wall, I'll send my son to check on you. I'm so proud of him. He's a linebacker on his high school team and at the top of his class. He wants to be a state trooper. Let's get you registered."

After I signed in, she took my credit card and stared at the registration. "Karen O'Brien? Did you used to go to school here? Karen O'Brien was one of my oldest sister's friends. My sister, Evangeline, but we called her Angel, bless her soul, used to say Karen O'Brien was the smartest girl she knew. That was you, wasn't it?"

My eyes widened. "I remember Angel. She was a force. I'm sure you know that. I'm so sorry to hear she passed."

"Thank you. I still miss her. Angel died from smoke inhalation and burn injuries after she tried to save a family in a house fire."

I nodded and sipped my coffee. "That's the Angel I knew."

"Here I am, going on, and I haven't even introduced myself. I'm Devlin. Angel named me. She told our mother Devlin meant brave, but I'm sure you can guess what Angel called me." She laughed as she pointed to a flyer and form on the registration desk.

"Have you eaten? We order meals from a diner that delivers. Here's the menu and order form. Mark what you want and your room number and come to the office at seven this evening to pick up your food. We have coffee and donuts for our visitors in the morning. We get donuts from the shop in town. Best in the state."

After I turned in my dinner form, I rolled my suitcase to my room. The furnishings were old but gleamed. The linens on the double bed were spotless, and the porcelain on the tub was chipped, but the bathroom sparkled.

I picked up the receiver of the old-style landline phone in my room and called Shirley. Her phone rolled to voice mail, and I sighed in relief. "This is Karen. Slight change of plans. Pick me up in the morning at nine at the Asbury Motel."

I kicked off my shoes and sunk into the seat of the overstuffed chair. I grinned and patted the chair's arm.

"It's okay. My springs aren't as strong as they used to be either."

When I picked up my meal at seven, Devlin said, "Don't forget coffee and donuts in the morning."

I'd ordered baked chicken, macaroni and cheese, collards, and a dinner roll. When I opened my takeout sack, my stomach rumbled in appreciation of the tantalizing aroma of sweet basil, sharp cheese, and smoked bacon. I discovered the additions of sweet tea and a slice of pecan pie. *This is home.*

I woke at six and jumped into the shower then dressed. When I opened the door to the office, two children with donuts in each of their hands dashed past me. A young woman raced after them. "Sorry," she called over her shoulder.

I lined up behind four other guests for a cup of coffee. After I poured my coffee, I stepped out of the way to enjoy the morning excitement without being trampled.

A couple who were my age joined me.

"Lovely place, isn't it?" the woman asked. "Our friend from Atlanta told us to stay here. I thought she was nuts when we drove up to the motel."

"You told me to keep driving," her husband said.

"Not in so many words."

"Yes, you did."

"I believe I said we could make it to Atlanta by midnight, but I'm glad you turned off your hearing aid," she chuckled. "This is the most relaxing place we've ever stayed."

I nodded. "I slept better last night than I've slept in years."

The man disposed of their trash. "Ready?" They waved as they left.

Devlin joined me at my personal observation point. "Care for a donut?"

"I need my quota of coffee first."

"You here for a visit?" she asked. "Don't mean to pry, sorry."

"No, it's fine. My plan is to move back to Asbury."

"Sounds wonderful. Excuse me." Devlin hurried to the desk where a man waited to check out.

I drank my second cup then returned to my room to pack and relax before Shirley appeared; she pulled into the motel parking lot right on time.

"The furniture store opens at nine," she said. "Did you want to go by the house again first? Is there anything else you need?"

"I'll need internet service and a laptop and printer," I said.

"We'll change the utilities to your name, and you'll need groceries. We should be able to get all your shopping done by lunch if we don't dawdle."

The organization of the furniture store reminded me of a warehouse with groups of similar furniture pieces together. To our left were sofas of all styles, fabrics, and size. To our right were overstuffed chairs with recliners at a midpoint in the building. Each group had gleaming end tables or coffee tables interspersed with the furniture pieces. *Who dusts all the tables?*

We wandered inside, and I ran my hand along the soft fabric on a sofa. A salesman stepped in our path. "Help you?"

"I need a mattress set and a bedframe," I said.

"Back here." He weaved his way to the back of the store and to the right, and we trailed along behind him.

The twin-size mattresses were twice as wide and two feet longer than my mat in prison.

"We arrange the mattresses by size," the salesman said.

I patted a twin mattress. "This will work."

"Most of our customers buy a queen or king bed." The salesman pointed down the line to the larger mattresses that would have filled my cell.

"You can't get a twin," Shirley said.

"Why is that?" I asked.

"Your bedroom is too big for a twin bed." Shirley stepped to the next larger size.

I frowned. "That makes no sense."

"We can compromise with a double bed," she said. "I don't think you need a king."

I shook my head. "How is that a compromise?"

"You wouldn't be happy with a king size. A double is a good compromise."

"Your mattress. Soft or hard?" the salesman asked.

I wandered down the row of mattresses and squinted at each one. *I have no clue.* "This one." I pointed to the mattress and box spring set marked *medium*.

"Do you want a fabric headboard or wooden? I like fabric." Shirley examined the fabric headboards and rubbed the satin fabric with her fingertips.

"No headboard," I said.

"But this one is nice." She ran her hand over a blue tufted headboard.

"How about this one?" I pointed to a solid rose quilted headboard.

"But the color. Nothing goes with that dark pink." Shirley shuddered.

"It's more of a rose," I said.

The salesman nodded. "Rose is closer to red on the color spectrum than it is to pink and is the newest color this year."

Shirley tapped her fingers on the rose headboard. "We'll think about it. When can you deliver the bed?"

The salesman flipped open his folder. "I can schedule it for this afternoon."

"We'll take it if the store can deliver and set it up this afternoon."

On the way to the register, Shirley said, "If we got that pink headboard, we could always have it recovered later when we're tired of the color. Maybe we'll come back for it when it goes on sale. Nobody else would buy it."

We? I rolled my eyes.

After we changed the utilities and set up my internet service, Shirley parked at the electronics store. "I'll just wait here. I don't know anything about computers."

When I approached the door, a middle-aged man opened it. "You must be Karen O'Brien. I'm Max.

Welcome to Asbury. Or maybe I should say welcome back to Asbury. How can I help you?"

"I need a laptop, software, and a printer. My internet will be set up in a day or so."

"Tell me how you plan to use your computer, and we'll pick one out for you."

"Documents and spreadsheets, internet searches, and maybe email. No games."

"This one will work for you." Max pointed to a laptop in the lower end of the price range of laptops. "And I'll install the software for you. It won't take long."

As he watched the screen, Max asked, "You here for good? Bet the town's changed a lot. I've only been in Asbury five years. Slow, sleepy town, but I like it. People are nice."

"Some new stores and old ones out of business, but not much change overall. Not sure if I could have stayed if Gus had closed up shop."

"Isn't that the truth?" Max chuckled.

Thirty minutes later, I carried my purchases out of the store.

"That didn't take long," Shirley said. "This works out great for me. I'm catching up on all my phone calls. You can pick up linens, your kitchen things, and groceries at the new super store. I have another call to make. I'll find you."

Shirley was still on the phone after I checked out and rolled my full cart to the parking lot. She hung up and jumped out of the car to help unload the cart.

"Now that I've caught up on all my calls, I have meetings all afternoon, but we could pick you up some lunch on the way to your house. I won't be able to stay. I'll eat on the run."

"I appreciate all your help, but I'll be fine. I bought lunch things at the grocery store."

When we reached the house, we carried my purchases inside then Shirley sped off to her meeting.

I placed my grocery items in the refrigerator, freezer, or pantry then shook my head. "Poor pantry. One can of corn looks lonely. I need to relearn how to shop."

I set the ingredients for a ham and cheese sandwich on the counter and rolled up my sleeves to wash my hands and create my sandwich. I toasted the bread, spread mayonnaise, added extra mustard, draped a piece of ham on one slice of bread so it fit on the bread, added cheese, and cut the bread into two triangles and examined my plate. *Extra mustard and swiss cheese. It's been twelve years since I made a sandwich.*

After lunch, I placed dishes, silverware, and pots in the dishwasher and cleaned the kitchen cabinets while the dishwasher ran. I sniffed my clothes and coughed at the diesel and sour body odor from the bus. I tossed all my clothes except what I was wearing into the washer. After the first load finished, I started another one with the bed linens I'd bought. The third load was towels and the new blanket.

When my new bed arrived, the two delivery men set it up for me. After they left, I made the bed with the fresh sheets and new quilt then stood at the doorway and scanned my room. *My bedroom.* I sat on my bed with a book on my lap, and tears slipped down my face. *I'm home.* I fluffed my pillow and propped it against the wall to read. *Maybe I should get the rose headboard.*

I woke with a start and stared wide-eyed at my surroundings until I realized where I was. *My room. My house. I'm safe.* I slowed my breathing and stretched.

I stepped outside onto my back porch and shaded my eyes with my arm. *Sun's bright.* The birds sang songs celebrating the clear skies. The previous owners had a bird feeder in the backyard, but it was empty. *I need birdseed.* I dropped my wallet into my backpack and strolled to the hardware store in town.

When I reached the hardware store, a woman behind the counter smiled. "Ms. O'Brien? Can I help you find something?"

"I need birdseed for a feeder at my house. What do you suggest?"

"Let's start you with a small bag of our most popular feed. It's sunflower, pumpkin, and a mix of smaller seeds. You can see how it works for the birds in your neighborhood. Does your house also have a bird bath or fountain? You'll want to keep it full of fresh water. If you don't have one, come back sometime, and we can talk about what would be the easiest for you to maintain."

On my way to the register, a clear container with a red lid caught my attention. "Is this large enough to hold the bird seed?"

"It's close, but after you fill your feeder, it should be fine. That's a good idea. You can keep your birdseed on a shelf without accidental spills to clean up."

I hurried home with my birdseed and container. I filled the birdfeeder and poured the rest of the sack into my new container then lurked at the kitchen window to see if the birds liked the seeds. After a half-hour, I realized the birds needed a chance to discover the seeds in the bird feeder.

My plan was to scrub a potato and wrap it in foil to bake in the oven for supper, but it was another half-hour before my potato was in the oven because I kept checking the bird feeder. I slathered a chicken breast with sauce and placed it in the oven then rewarded myself with another bird feeder peek.

"There's a bird." I applauded my first visitor, and the shadows danced in the hallway.

I took my book to the back porch to read and peek at the bird feeder as birds flitted in to check for seeds. The larger birds that knocked small seeds to the ground and the smaller birds that picked through the seeds in the grass mesmerized me.

An hour later, I set my silverware and napkin on the counter where I could see the bird feeder. I plated my food then stabbed a bite of potato. "I'm obsessed over the birds because they're free. I'm not sure I've realized I am too." I glanced around. No shadows. *Guess I'm talking to myself.*

After I ate, I strolled to the park four blocks away. The azaleas and roses gave the surrounding neighborhoods a beauty and fragrance I hadn't experienced in years, and tears slid down my cheeks. I relaxed on a park bench while the squirrels chattered and chased each other from tree to tree. I returned home by a longer route and stopped in front of a house with a garden of butterfly bush, cosmos, lantana, and lilac, and a host of butterflies dipping into the flowers. *This is why I came home.* I rolled my eyes. *Still talking to myself.*

When I woke early the next morning, I was grateful I remembered where I was. I perked a pot of coffee and sipped a cup while I stared at Shorty's addresses. *Maybe if I draw a US map and mark the relative locations and number them, I'll see a pattern.*

After the morning sun filled the backyard with its warm rays, I searched for a forgotten bird bath. I was almost sad when I found one intact with its pedestal. *I had my heart set on a bubbling fountain.* I set the bird bath upright and went inside for cleaning material. I scrubbed, rinsed, then placed the bird bath close to the bird feeder before I hauled water to fill it. *I need a garden hose.*

I hurried inside and refilled my coffee cup. I sipped and developed lists for the grocery and hardware stores. The hardware store had a garden wagon. *I could use that for hauling groceries too.* I added a garden hose and a wagon to my hardware list.

I spent the morning shopping and the afternoon watering the sparse yard with my new garden hose. *I like this quiet life.*

The next day, the technician installed the internet and set up my laptop on wi-fi. After he left, I laid my

Christmas cards on the countertop while I searched the addresses I'd copied onto the cards. The first address was the sheriff's office in Knoxville, Tennessee. *Sheriff's office?* I checked the address and searched again. *I expected a residence or a business.*

The second address was the police department in Pittsburgh, Pennsylvania. The third address was the police department in Yakima, Washington. All the addresses were law enforcement offices in different areas of the United States. I stretched and turned off my computer. *I'll check the dates later.*

I strolled around the outside of my house. The previous owner had a lawn service mow the yard, but weeds had overrun the grass, and the bare, dried stems near the porch may have been flowers at one time. *Where do I start? Maybe Shirley's right about a landscaping service.*

After supper, I showered and snuggled in my bed with a new book. At midnight, I closed my book and turned off the overhead light.

The rumble of thunder woke me at five. I dressed and started a pot of coffee as the wind increased and the light showers turned to a downpour. I grabbed a peach yogurt and sipped my coffee as I powered up my laptop to check the weather. The radar showed the storm moving from the southwest.

"No rain after ten this morning, and the store scheduled my furniture delivery at two. We should be okay." I glanced at the hallway. *No shadows.*

While I was on the computer, I found a news station in Knoxville and scanned their archived news for the date range. The newsfeed flooded me with more data than I expected because the date range was too broad.

I checked the news in Ohio and didn't find anything about a murder in the women's prison, and I wondered about Duchess. *I don't know what her name is on the outside.*

That afternoon, Shirley dropped by as my stored furniture was being delivered. "You didn't have much in storage, did you? There's a nice thrift store in town. You may want to check it out. I've pulled the for-sale listings for businesses. Let me know when you want to talk to the owners. I have appointments tomorrow, but I can keep the next day free for you. There aren't that many businesses for sale in town, so it won't take you long to pick one or two to investigate. Let me know if your plans change."

She hurried to her car. *Bye, Shirley.*

My furniture had suffered from twelve years of being in storage and from being moved in then out of the warehouse. My dining table and chairs were dirty and musty, and parts and joints were broken or loose. I stared at my furniture. *Twelve years of neglect. Twelve years lost.*

Sadness then anger I didn't know I had boiled up and overwhelmed me. I grabbed my coffee cup off the counter and threw it against the wall. When it shattered, I covered my face with my hands and sobbed.

When I had no more tears left, I swept up the cup shards and cleaned the wall and floor. *I can clean and repair the furniture. A real test of my skills is can I repair myself?*

I traipsed to the hardware store for glue, screws, nails, clamps, two types of screwdrivers, and a hammer. I added a pair of tan leather gloves and a red toolbox on impulse before I checked out. When I returned home with my tools, I attacked the grime one piece at a time until my hands cramped.

I trudged to bed and grumbled. "My enthusiastic ambition exceeds the ability of my ancient bones to perform." The shadows in the hallway followed me then disappeared.

I awoke the next morning and leaped out of bed ready to tackle the furniture. *But first, coffee.*

After I dressed, I scrubbed the last three pieces of furniture then assessed each piece and planned the repairs.

At the end of the day, I was as grimy as my furniture had been. After my hot shower, I snuggled in bed with a book, and no one disturbed my new magic privacy bubble.

SWEET DEAL SEALED

By the end of the second morning, I'd cleaned, repaired, tightened, oiled, and polished my old furniture. I arranged the sparse furniture and admired my handiwork. *I might not have any landscaping talents, but the furniture looks great.*

After lunch, I strolled the mile and a half to Shirley's office to look at the business listings. I stopped along the way to enjoy the beauty of a neighbor's early blooming azaleas and inhaled the sweet floral perfume. The slight breeze and light cloud cover kept the humidity and heat low. I glanced at the sky. The gathering clouds promised late afternoon showers. *Maybe a thunderstorm. All those years wasted with no flowers, trees, grass, or the freedom to wander wherever my feet took me.* A tear slid down my cheek. I stared at a hawk overhead as it floated in large circles on the thermals. *Gliding in warm air above the earth. That's freedom.*

A small bird landed on a bush, chirped at me, and flitted to another branch in front of me. "Hi, bird." *I need a bird identification book to carry on my walks.*

Shirley's office was on the corner of Main Street and shared an old building with three other businesses. When I stepped inside, Shirley was on the phone at her desk in the back of the office. She waved and continued her conversation. The low white ceiling tiles and the faux-wood paneling hid the building's unique architectural personality. The narrow office had a corkboard with photos of properties for sale and metal file cabinets lined up on the left and single pane windows on the right that overlooked the side street.

Shirley hung up and pointed to a single sheet of paper on the front desk. "That's my real estate partner's desk. She isn't active as far as selling, but she's our local association president and keeps her license current. That sheet's a list of businesses for you. I have one more quick call to make."

The desk was bare, not even a phone, except for a collection of framed cross-stitched real estate sayings. I picked them up one by one to read the sayings. I grinned at Mark Twain's *Buy Land. They aren't making it anymore.*

I read the short list of businesses for sale. *Moving company, no. Auto repair, no. Donut shop sounds nice.*

I glanced at Shirley. *Still on the phone.*

I scooted the chair away from the desk to sit and stopped. *For the past twelve years, I've waited for somebody to tell me what to do. No more.*

I cleared my throat and held up the paper. "I found something interesting."

She ended her conversation, rushed to the front, and frowned. "Well, if you're sure. I'll make a quick call and arrange for us to visit."

After the call, Shirley grabbed her overstuffed purse and pulled out her keys. My eyes widened. *She must be a magician.*

"Do you want to follow me? We can take my car, and you can ride with me. It isn't far. Let me lock up. I parked in the alley in the back. I thought you'd pick the mobile dog wash because..."

I interrupted. "Do you have a more detailed listing I could read on the way there?"

Shirley turned to her desk and slipped another sheet out of a stack.

I blinked and shook my head. *How does she do that?*

On our way, Shirley handed me a folder. "Just in case you aren't crazy about the donut shop. It's pretty old. New equipment would be a big expense. Here are some others we can look at while we're out. We'll find you something more to your liking."

When we stopped at a red light, Shirley narrowed her eyes and tapped the steering wheel. "Karen, did you know your hair's more gray than brown now? I'll make an appointment for you to get a touch-up and a more current cut."

"I'm fine."

Shirley snorted. "No, you're not. Everybody knows we're the same age. You can't wander around town looking older than we are."

I smiled at the Shirley-logic.

When I stepped out of Shirley's car, my eyes widened, and my heart filled with joy at the sight of the old building. The sign over the door, *The Donut Hole*, was hand-crafted. I opened the shop door and stopped to soak up the wooden floors, the patina of the oak counter and its stools, and the sturdy equipment. I was mesmerized by the sweet smell of donuts and pastries and the timeless beauty of the old shop. I stared at the tin ceiling and glanced over my shoulder. Shirley's two-year-old car was still at the curb.

I snorted. *I just checked to make sure we hadn't fallen into a time warp.*

Chapter Three

Shirley pushed past me and grumbled. "What's wrong with you? Change your mind? Come on in."

A wizened man who was at least three inches shorter than me scurried out of a back room. His sparse gray hair stood out in all directions like it had been static-charged in an electricity experiment. "Name's Otto Rothenberger. People call me Donut Man."

He brushed his gnarled hands on his apron, and we shook hands. A black and tan German shepherd ambled to my side. The dog had amber eyes, a black face with a little gray around his muzzle, gray around his neck, and a saddle of black across his back. His tail, legs, and chest were light and dark shades of tan. I held out my hand for a sniff and was rewarded with a lick. I saw a gray tail flick and disappear around the counter.

Mr. Rothenberger grinned. "This here's Colonel, and there goes my cat, Mia. I think they like you."

"My kids signed me up for a nursing home," he said as I peeked into the stockroom. "They call it something fancier, but I can't take my animals. My dog and cat need to stay with the shop."

"I love the charm of your shop, and Colonel and Mia are part of the charm, aren't they?"

Shirley sniffed. I glowered at her. *You liked animals when we were kids.*

I took the old man's arm, and we walked to the counter. "We can work something out," I said.

Shirley slammed the door when she left.

"Yep, dog and cat along with all my recipes." He grinned.

I smiled. "I stayed at the Asbury Motel my first night in town. Do their donuts come from your shop?"

"Sure do. I took donuts to the Asbury Motel the first morning they were open. Angel and Devlin were little things back then. I used to deliver, but I got too old for all that running around. Devlin or her son drop by around lunchtime and pick up their donuts for the next day. Devlin says she's never had a complaint about freshness. I think she does some storing magic."

"I thought they'd come straight out of the fryer. Thank you for everything. I never thought about owning a donut shop, but it might be a good fit."

"Just let me know," he said, and we shook hands.

Shirley was in her car. She handed me a sheet when I got in.

"This is the mobile dog wash. If it isn't the right business for you, I have another one you might like." She handed me another sheet. "The auto repair has been very successful. You were handy when we were kids. This might be up your alley."

I read the sheet. "This is a one-man shop, Shirley. I'm not a trained mechanic."

"You were the smartest girl in our class. I'm sure you could learn. Lots of people learn new things all the time. I learned the new computer system for agents. Well, I almost learned; at least I sat through the training. I still need a little help. Not much. Only when I have to put in a new listing or change one and sometimes when I want to run a report. The changes I put in never show up online, but a high school girl drops by my office on her way home from school and takes care of things on the computer for me. I pay her so she'll keep helping me. Doreen keeps trying to take her away from me. I told Doreen..."

"I've made up my mind. If I'm going to learn something new, I want to learn how to make donuts."

Shirley frowned. "The donut shop doesn't make as much money as the auto repair, and donuts will make you fat. I don't think that's a good idea."

"You know the auto repair owner, right? Who's fatter? The auto repair owner or Mr. Rothenberger?"

Shirley stared at me. "Never thought of it like that before. Auto repair makes a person fat. Who knew? I always knew you were the smartest girl in our class."

I hid my smile. *Maybe the best guesser.*

"Where do we go next?" Shirley asked. "The dog wash? There's also the landscaping business. Do you think you'd like to do landscaping? I don't have the spec sheet for it yet. I hear the boutique might come on the market soon too. Would you like that? You could learn some fashion sense. That's something useful you need to learn. I could help you. There are magazines you could rcad. Maybe you'd like to take some design classes while we wait for it. We could ask the owner what courses would be best for you to start with."

"Donut shop, Shirley."

"Sleep on it. If you don't change your mind, come see me tomorrow, but no animals."

Early the next morning, I ate my yogurt in front of my back window to watch birds then hurried to Shirley's office and waited.

Shirley unlocked her door forty-five minutes after I arrived.

She glowered. "Did you stand out here all night? It's a wonder you weren't arrested for loitering except I don't think the sheriff would arrest you. Come in. Did you come to tell me you changed your mind about the donut shop?"

"I didn't change my mind." I followed her into her office.

"I made you a hair appointment for nine tomorrow. You don't have to agree to keep the dog and cat. I'm sure someone will take them. That's what animal shelters are for."

"Most of the women I knew in prison left children behind with the siblings split up among various relatives and foster care. Heartbreaking stories. I couldn't help them, but I can keep a dog and cat together. They belong in the shop. What's wrong with you?" I crossed my arms and glared.

"What are you talking about, what's wrong with me? Real estate transactions don't include animals. What's wrong with you?" She glared back.

"I'm going for a walk." I slammed the door as I left and power-walked around the block. When I returned, Shirley scowled as she stood in her doorway.

"Let's start over. I like the animals, and they like me. We'll be fine," I said. "And don't you love the business model? Open early and close mid-morning when all the pastries are gone. It's perfect for a retiree who's an early riser. What's more fulfilling than selling hot donuts first thing in the morning to other early risers?"

"It will take me a little while to prepare your offer then after you sign it, I'll take it to Mr. Otto." Shirley sighed.

"Colonel and Mia don't need to be in the real estate transaction but tell Mr. Rothenberger I'll keep them."

Shirley headed into the office. "You should tell him yourself. I do real estate. Are you in a hurry? I'm not fast with the new computer forms. You want to wait here or somewhere else?"

"I'll hang around in case you have any questions. I brought along a book to read." *And so you won't get distracted by phone calls.*

I settled in at the front desk to read while Shirley muttered to her computer. Two hours later, Shirley rose from her desk. "I think I've got it. I'll print it, and you can check it for me."

I read through the offer. "Looks good to me."

After I initialed and signed the document, Shirley said, "Why don't you meet me at Ida's Diner in a half-hour? I don't think it will take any longer than that to present the offer to Mr. Otto. Ida's is the most popular place for lunch with the downtown office crowd. My treat. If they have cherry pie, tell them to set aside a piece for me. Text me if the special is meatloaf. I need your cell phone number. I gotta scoot. I'm parked in back."

After living in Ohio for thirty years, I'd forgotten the southern custom of referring to our elders as Mr. or Ms. with their first names. The words sounded quaint for a brief second, but not so out of place with the addition of the soft drawl. *I'll have my drawl back in less than a month.*

I window-shopped on my way to the diner, but I didn't have time to go into the bookstore or stop by the hardware store. *Wonder if Ida's ever changed owners?* Maybe I could get some ideas from the manager or owner, like whether I should change the name of the donut shop.

Shirley pulled to the curb and rolled down the passenger window. "Come on, get in. Mr. Otto wants to talk to you. He's accepted your offer but wanted you there when he signed the papers. I need your phone number. I could have called you. I'll drop you off and be back to pick up the papers. Fifteen minutes." *I suppose I should get a cell phone.*

When I walked into the donut shop, Mr. Otto sat at the counter with the signed papers. Colonel greeted me, and I rubbed his face. Mia paraded out from the storeroom. I was struck by her green eyes, her glitter-gray coat, and the tip of white on her left paw. She surveyed the shop, her kingdom, gave me a regal nod, and disappeared behind the counter.

Mr. Otto handed me his business card with a phone number handwritten on the back. "I wanted to thank you. You're the perfect owner for the donut shop. All my recipes are in a binder in the freezer, but if you don't understand any of them or want to discuss an idea, call me."

I brushed a sneaky tear away from my cheek. "Thank you. It's perfect. Old dog, old cat, old shop, for an old lady."

We shook hands and hugged. Deal sealed, and I was a business owner.

Now I just need to learn how to make donuts.

"I might need a few lessons. Can I work with you the rest of the week?"

The next morning, I met Mr. Rothenberger at the shop at five-thirty.

"I got here early to organize everything for your first lesson. Today I'll walk you through the steps then I'll be your assistant starting tomorrow."

I swallowed hard then rushed to wash my hands. By the end of the morning, I was covered in flour and drained.

"You did great, Karen. I'm impressed by how quickly you caught on. Do you feel like you ran a marathon? I'm derelict in my duties. I forgot to get you a medal." Mr. Rothenberger chuckled and patted my hand.

"What time do you come to the shop?" I asked.

"I'm here by four-thirty."

"See you in the morning."

After I left the shop, I limped home and relaxed with my book. When I awoke, I stretched and carried my lunch yogurt to the back porch to watch the birds. A female cardinal perched on the birdfeeder and pecked at the seed. She ate the sunflower seeds and knocked the smaller seeds to the ground. A bright-red male cardinal stood guard on the nearby fence.

I power-walked to the bookstore then bought two new books as my reward for remembering to exercise. That evening, I snuggled on my sofa and stressed over which book to read first. *Best kind of stress.* I closed my eyes and picked a book.

When I arrived at the shop the next morning at four-thirty, Mr. Rothenberger waited at the door. "What's your plan for today?" he asked.

"I'd like to make the glazed and maple donuts again and cranberry-orange scones."

"Classics first. Good. You work. I'll applaud, make positive comments, and keep the coffee pots full." Mr. Otto poured himself a cup of coffee and sat at the counter.

At the end of the morning, Mr. Otto asked, "How do you feel today?"

"Not so exhausted." I brushed the flour off my apron. "I'm not as floured as I was yesterday too. That's a good sign, right?"

"Very good sign."

At the end of the second week of my training, Mr. Otto and I reviewed his prior five years of sales records and expenses and developed a tentative production plan for my first month. His accountant came to the shop, and we spent a half day going over the taxes for the previous five years.

"This is it, Karen." Mr. Rothenberger shook my hand. "You'll be fine. Remember you can call me any time, but you don't need me. You're a talented baker. A natural. Work on that confidence and don't let the biddies get you down. Some use a different 'B' word." He winked.

"Mr. Rothenberger!" I laughed.

"They'll try. Just remember, you're talented."

After Mr. Rothenberger left, Colonel nudged my hand. "Are you going home with me, Colonel?"

He trotted to the front door and waited. I paused before I opened the door.

"What about you, Mia? Are you going or staying?"

Mia flicked her tail and marched to the storeroom.

When Colonel and I reached my house, I let him out of the car, and he explored the yard. After we went inside, he checked every room then flopped on the kitchen floor with a grin.

I filled a mixing bowl with water for him. "We need to get you and Mia food and food and water bowls, and Mia will need a box here. Want a drink? Then we'll go shopping."

I pulled the wagon to the hardware store. Colonel explored along the way but stayed close to me.

We went into the hardware store for our purchases then headed to the grocery store. Colonel waited outside with the wagon when I went inside with a grocery cart. *Ironic. I stressed over leaving rags inside my motel room, and I'm leaving a wagonful of purchases outside here.*

I added canned pinto beans to my cart before I checked out.

The cashier smiled as she took my cash. "I heard you bought Mr. Otto's shop. I see you've also inherited Colonel and Mia. Welcome home."

"Thank you." I returned her smile. *Small town news still travels fast.*

Colonel pranced as he led the way to his new home. I beamed. *I feel like prancing too.* I snorted. "Except I'm pulling the wagon. That's my excuse, Colonel."

I woke with a start on Monday morning and checked the clock. *Three o'clock.* It was my first day to run the donut shop solo. *No way will I sleep now.* I jumped out of bed, and Colonel stretched and followed me to the kitchen. I put on a pot of coffee and fed Colonel then let him out for his morning break. I gulped a cup of fresh coffee and burned the roof of my mouth. I cooled my mouth with my peach yogurt. After I let Colonel inside, I showered and dressed.

I checked the clock. *Three-thirty.*

"We might as well go to the shop, Colonel. I can be a nervous wreck there as easily as I can here."

The full moon in the cloudless sky lit our way through the neighborhoods to the shop. Traffic on the highway two miles away hummed, and the tree frogs and katydids chirped, and the light breeze kept the mosquitos away.

When we reached the shop, I unlocked the door and switched on the lights. After I locked the door behind us, the beauty of the old shop mesmerized me. Mia broke my trance as she meowed her complaint about the hour.

"Mr. Otto suggested we stick to the popular donuts today, pink-sprinkled and maple. He said we might want to celebrate a new owner with a new scone for the week. I was thinking maybe a rocky road scone. We're here early enough that I can make some to see how they work out."

Colonel grinned and flopped on the floor.

I returned from the freezer with Mr. Otto's recipe book and flipped through until I found the rocky road scone recipe. "Ha. I knew I'd find it here."

Mia stalked Colonel, and I gazed at my animals. "I'd be lonely if you two weren't in my life. I've never been alone. I went from my parents' home to the college dormitory then I was married. And I was certainly never alone in prison." I frowned. "Maybe I've really been alone my entire life while I lived with people who were strangers." I shook off my melancholy and turned back to the recipe book.

"Rocky road. Chocolate, marshmallows, and nuts. There are miniature marshmallows in the freezer. We're set."

I made a small batch of rocky road scones. "First ten customers get a free scone. What do you think?"

I mixed and set aside the dough to rise for my first two batches of donuts. "Thank goodness Mr. Otto was hands-off. I'd be freaking if I'd never done this by myself before now."

While the dough rose, I set up coffee to be started later. I monitored the clock as I fried donuts and donut holes and baked cranberry-orange scones.

When I lifted my first batch of donuts out of the fryer, I glanced at the window. The shadows were slinking in one corner, but another figure caught my attention, and I dropped the fryer basket onto the screen that drained the fried dough. I stared again at the window in time to see a small form scurry away. *Was that a child?*

At six-thirty, Shirley tapped on the door, and I hurried to let her in.

"I will never be here this early again. Just letting you know. Did you have to stay here all night to make donuts and scones? The shop smells wonderful. Maple donuts and cranberry-orange scones. Am I right? You need to write that on your board." Shirley inhaled. "I smell fresh coffee. I like the largest size for my to-go and lots of sugar. The only reason I got up early was to be your first customer. Am I your first customer? Do I get a special reward?"

I handed Shirley her coffee. "What would you like? Your special reward is a free scone."

"A maple donut and a free scone. I'm so excited for you. I knew you were perfect for the donut shop."

I snorted as I wrapped her donut and scone and slipped them into a white sack.

Mia stalked Shirley, and Shirley pointed her finger at Mia. "Don't even think about pouncing, cat." Colonel nudged Shirley's hand. "Hello, dog."

I handed Shirley her sack, and she put money on the counter before she dashed to the door. "I'll need a nap before I go into the office. I have a meeting at nine."

Sheriff Grady Hayes sauntered in not long after Shirley left and peered into the display case. He was tall and lean, and his face had the kindness of farmers and crossing guards. His dark-brown hair was short and neat, except for his out-of-control cowlick. His brown shirt and pants were pressed with crisp creases.

"Your first day without Mr. Otto? Coffee smells fresh. What do you recommend?" he asked.

I poured a cup of coffee and set it on the counter. "I have pink-sprinkled donuts, maple donuts, cranberry-orange scones, and a free treat for my first ten customers, rocky road scones."

The sheriff burst into a hearty laugh as he sat and drank his coffee. "Is that like *break a leg* for the theater crowd? I'll take one of each. Got to support my local donut lady."

I put all four pastries on a plate and poured a second cup of coffee for me.

"This your first break? What time did you come in?"

I refilled his cup and chuckled as I sat on the stool next to him. "I was here much too early, but only because I couldn't sleep. Opening day jitters."

He held up the pink-sprinkled donut. "This little gem is my favorite." He munched it down in four bites. "I gotta try that rocky road next."

His radio crackled, and he rose. "Duty calls."

I grabbed a white sack and dropped his donut and scones into it before he dashed out the door.

The bell over the door jingled, and I smiled at my next customer, Max. "Had to come see you." He inhaled. "I smell fresh-fried donuts, and did you bake something with oranges? Just walking in here made my mouth water. What do you recommend?"

"I have pink-sprinkled donuts, maple donuts, cranberry-orange scones, and a free rocky road scone to celebrate the shop under new ownership."

"Rocky road?" Max laughed. "Love it. I need one of everything, and I've traveled that particular road myself. Thank you. And coffee to go."

When Devlin came in, I gave her my last three free scones, and she carried out her three dozen donuts. At the end of the morning, I had leftover donuts. I checked Mr. Otto's notes. *No surprise. He never had leftovers.* I wrapped them individually then froze them.

"I don't know what else to do. I'm not sure how well they'll survive frozen. I'll research when we get home. You want to go with us, Mia?"

Mia scampered to the storeroom, and Colonel nosed the front door.

Toward the end of the first week after I took over the bakery as a solo, I counted the donuts at noon. I sold less than half the donuts I'd made, even after Devlin's order. I had ten dozen donuts in the freezer. *What do I do now?*

I reviewed the plan Mr. Otto and I had developed, and my stomach churned. "Mr. Otto and I thought we'd adjusted for a new owner, but this is way off. I can't afford to lose this much in one week. How much do I cut back on production? I hate to call Mr. Otto. He said there might be a little snubbing because I'm…" I cleared my throat, and my eyes welled up "…an ex-con." Colonel nudged my elbow, and I scratched his ears.

I brushed at a tear on my cheek and rubbed my forehead. "Buying a business in Asbury was a terrible idea. Should I ask Shirley if she put a thirty-day return clause in my purchase or something? Is that even possible? Why did I even think I could make a life here?"

Mia stalked Colonel then jumped on my lap. I stroked her back while I adjusted my plan for the next week by twenty percent and leaned back in my office chair. "Let's see how this works out." Mia jumped off my lap and dashed out of the storeroom that doubled as my office.

I gazed at the display case. "No sense in letting these go to waste, right, Colonel?"

Colonel and I walked to the soup kitchen with three dozen donuts. When we were inside, I called out, "Hello? Hello?"

An elderly woman rushed through the kitchen door.

"I'm Karen." I held out my hand, and she stared at me.

I cleared my throat and returned my hand to holding the boxes. "I bought the Donut Hole from Mr. R. I am learning the system and made too many donuts today. I'd like to share with your clients."

"I don't know…"

"Well, we can just leave these here." I placed the donuts on the nearest table, and Colonel and I left.

"I suppose there's a process for donations," I said on the way back to the shop.

When I walked past the Soup Kitchen later in the day on my way to the grocery store, I saw my donuts in the dumpster. My heart sunk.

Okay, Mr. Otto. I'm talented.

I marched into the soup kitchen. A tall volunteer in her early fifties with bleached blond hair elbowed a woman who was much shorter and twenty years older than she was. The tall woman sniffed and inclined her head toward me. The two of them skittered out. I sauntered in and surveyed the kitchen. *Stove needs cleaning.*

A slender woman in her early fifties who had brown hair streaked with gray came into the kitchen. Her nametag said *Director*. "May I help you?"

"Are you the manager?" I asked.

"I'm the director." She raised an eyebrow. "Is there something I can do for you?"

"I'm not sure we've met. I'm Karen O'Brien." I held out my hand.

She turned her back on me and walked to the stove. "I know who you are. What are you doing here? Need a handout?"

"Yes, I do. You mean a hand up, right? I do need some help."

"I'll have the social worker contact you." She headed to the door.

I squared my shoulders and lifted my chin. "Have you ever heard the expression, *Don't let the biddies get you down?*"

She froze. "Excuse me?" She wheeled around and stared. "Mr. Otto told you that, didn't he? He told me the same thing when I came here ten years ago."

I snickered. "Seriously? You mean there's a secret society of us outcasts?"

She sat on a stool and laughed. "You win, Donut Lady. I might have to knock some heads together, but no more donuts in the dumpster. By the way, I sneaked one, and it was delicious. Thank you for giving an old man a much-deserved opportunity to retire. I'm Melinda Wallace. Nice to meet a fellow outcast." She held out her hand, and we shook.

Early Monday morning I checked the scones in the oven, and the mingled aroma of hot pastry, cranberry, and orange swirled around me. *Ahh. Sweetness infusion.* I moved the lightly browned scones to the cooling rack and pulled the last two baskets of donuts and donut holes out of the fryer and tossed them onto the wire mesh screen to drain.

A quick glance at the clock showed thirty minutes until opening, which was plenty of time to mix the orange drizzle for the scones and the chocolate glaze for the donuts. I brushed my flour-covered hands on my signature pink apron. "Remind me to buy some white aprons to wear while I bake, Mia."

Mia opened one feline eye, swished her tail in disdain, and went back to sleep. Colonel wagged his curled, bushy tail.

"Fine. Colonel will remind me."

I emptied the commercial dishwasher and stacked my plates with the small pink sprinkled donut in the middle. The accountant had complained about a frivolous expense, but I told her it was my marketing plan. *Like I even know anything about marketing.* Guess I better let her know about the coffee cups I've ordered with pink sprinkles and *Got Sprinkles?* on the side before she gets the invoice.

I sprayed the countertop with my cleaning mixture of vinegar and water and buffed until it gleamed. I glanced out the large front window. The sun peeked over the horizon and revealed the scrawny boy who stood at the window. He remained still and stared at the display case. *Was his scowl because he couldn't see in the case or because he was hungry? My experience said hungry.*

I spotted the boy almost every day about this time. When he noticed I'd seen him, he'd hurry away. Today he lingered.

I set my spray bottle and cleaning rag under the counter. I guessed the boy was about eight or nine. *Always alone so early. Why?*

On impulse, I hurried to open the door before he disappeared. The old bell above the door jingled to announce my first customer of the day. "Hi, come on in."

His eyes narrowed. "Really?"

I know that suspicious look. Never saw it on anyone so young, though.

"Sure. Come on in. I've got work to do before I can open the store, and a little company would be nice."

The boy stepped inside and examined the shop with his muscles tensed. *A feral cat ready to scoot for cover.*

His jeans were short for him; they ended above his ankles. His faded green T-shirt was a few sizes too big and frayed at the neck. Insect bites marked the dark-brown skin on his arms and neck. He smelled sour, like bathing was not a routine for him. His gaunt face, sunken dark eyes, and bony arms and legs looked like regular meals were not on his schedule either.

I turned away to drizzle the chocolate frosting on a tray of donuts. "Make yourself comfortable at the counter."

I sneaked a peek, and the boy stood next to the stool closest to the door while Colonel leaned against his leg. The boy rubbed the dog's ear.

I drizzled and admired my handiwork. "You like donuts?"

"Don't have no money," he growled.

I turned to put the donuts in the display case and when I glanced up, he eased toward the door. I set the donut tray down and rubbed my chin. "Ever heard of barter?"

He looked at the floor, and I waited for his response. "Never hearda barter."

"That's when two people exchange something of value with each other but don't use money. Both parties benefit."

The scowl was back.

"So, for example, I need this floor swept before the shop opens. If you sweep it, I'll give you two donuts and a glass of milk. Deal?"

I smiled while he searched my face. His doubt faded.

"Deal." We shook hands.

I waved at the broom and the dustpan in the back of the shop. I wiped fingerprints off the display glass and watched while he swept without stirring up any dust. *Someone has taught him to clean.*

When he finished, he put the broom and dustpan away. I inspected the floor and nodded. *No dirt in the corners. No dust under the counter. Outstanding.*

"Well done. I'll get you a glass of milk. You decide which two donuts you want."

When I returned with the milk, the boy was peering through the display glass at the donuts. "I don't know."

"How about a maple? And a classic glazed."

He nodded, and I placed the two donuts on a plate at the counter with the milk. The boy washed his hands at the staff sink. I raised my eyebrows. Somebody had taught him to scrub his hands before he ate, but he apparently didn't have access to regular bathing facilities.

He climbed up on the stool at the counter. "Ain'tcha gonna eat too?"

"I have to open the shop."

He nodded, folded his hands, and placed them in his lap. "Okay."

I didn't expect that, but it would be rude to refuse to eat with him. "Give me a minute to flip the sign to *Open* and pour a cup of coffee."

I set my coffee and a plate with my maple donut on the counter next to him.

The boy bowed his head. "Bless these donuts."

More surprises. Where are these people who love him?

"Amen." I cringed a little and wondered if God cringed too.

I took a bite of my maple donut. The sweet maple flavor swirled on my tongue like warm maple syrup. "Oh yum, this is good. I've never had a maple donut. Pleasantly creamy and not overbearing. Gooey. Why have I never stopped to eat a warm donut before?" *What else am I missing?*

"Yumph," A mouthful of donut muffled his voice.

After we ate, he hopped off his stool. "I like barter."

I smiled. "Thank you for sweeping."

He turned to wave as he hurried away. I put my hand up and paused. *I've lost all my social skills. I forgot to ask his name.*

I rinsed our dishes and put them in the dishwasher. The bell jingled, and a young man in a dark gray suit, a white shirt, and a red tie strode to the counter.

He grinned. "I'm Dustin. I'm here because I was promoted to sales manager at the car dealership. My wife bought me this new suit for my first staff meeting." He frowned. "It's not too much, is it? I need three dozen celebration donuts."

"Your suit is nice. Managerial. You want a mix, all the same, or do you want to choose?"

His eyes widened. "A mix, is that okay?"

"You're the boss man." I smiled.

He cleared his throat and straightened his shoulders. "A mix. Three dozen. Please."

After the happy sales manager left, a woman rushed in, out of breath. She had pulled her dark hair onto the top of her head into a messy ponytail, and she wore black yoga pants and an oversized Georgia Bulldogs T-shirt. "We had a miscommunication. I thought my turn was next month. I need a dozen scones for my book club. And some donut holes. My club says they don't eat donuts. I ignore their faulty logic. At least my cleaning people came to the house yesterday, or we'd meet in the street." She looked around. "Why don't you host book clubs here?"

I packaged up scones and donut holes while she talked. "I hadn't thought about it, but it might be an idea. Come back when you have time, and let's talk. Seems like you need this." I handed her a cup of coffee. "Black and sweet?"

She took a sip and smiled while she paid. "Perfect. Thanks."

SWEET DEAL SEALED

The sheriff opened the door for her as she left and strode into the shop. He frowned at the empty display case.

"Your uniform is always fresh. You must stop at the dry cleaners every morning and pick it up." I walked to the coffee pot and poured him a cup.

He beamed. "My wife takes care of me. She's the best."

"Have to warn you I'm still learning. I made too many donuts last week, and I might have cut back too much. I have only two sprinkle donuts left. Devlin already picked up her order, or we could borrow one from her."

"Been wanting a couple of your pink-sprinkled donuts all morning. My favorite." Grady devoured his first donut in three bites and gulped down his coffee while I cleaned inside the display case.

He peered into his empty mug. "Got any more?"

"I had company this morning." I refilled his cup. "A young boy wanders by the shop early every morning. Today I invited him in, and he swept the floor for a couple of donuts and milk."

"About ten years old? A little skinny? Black? Chip on his shoulder?" He polished off the rest of his second donut.

I scrubbed the baking sheets before I loaded them into the commercial dishwasher. "Yes. Yes. Yes. No chip."

"Well, for a minute there, I thought you were describing Haywood," he said.

The bell jingled as Shirley hurried in. She frowned at the empty display case. Shirley might be a pain, but she was my first customer when I took over the shop, and she stopped in every day without fail.

"All gone? Why don't you make more donuts, so you don't run out so early? Not even a donut hole left?"

I reached below the counter and pulled out the sack with the donut and scone I'd set aside for her. When I turned to the coffee pot, the sheriff caught my eye and winked. I snickered and poured Shirley's usual twenty-ounce to-go coffee with milk and sugar.

I grinned. "Good morning, Shirley."

She peeked in her sack. "Maple donut and a cranberry orange scone. Did I hear Haywood was here? Did you have any trouble? He's a hard case. Father gone. Mother gone. No family around here. Haywood lived with his father's parents until he was five."

She took a breath and a sip of coffee. I watched in amazement because she didn't choke. *Maybe she's not a magician. Maybe she's an alien.*

"Ooo, hot. The grandparents died in a house fire," Shirley continued. "You remember the old Carruthers house, don't you, Karen? They bought it right after you left for college. Oh my gosh. That's close to thirty-five years ago. Or is it forty? I don't want to think about it. Remember Angel from school? Did you know she ran inside the burning house and pulled the grandmother out? The fire moved too fast. No one could get to the grandfather. None of them survived. Tragic. The old family dog pulled Haywood out. The dog died later from the fire too."

She looked down. Mia rubbed against her legs. Shirley wiggled her fingers. "Go away, cat. Haywood lives with these people who are supposed to be distant relatives of the mother, but who knows. Their little granddaughter lives with them too. I don't know them, and I know everybody. Boy's a known troublemaker at school. Held back last year..."

I broke in. "I don't know about all that. I don't know what his name is, but this morning's boy was a hard worker and polite."

Shirley slapped her money on the counter and headed for the door with her coffee and sack. "You need to save me an extra donut." She slammed the door as she left, and the bell jingled.

"Well, your visitor isn't the Haywood I know. More coffee?" Sheriff held up his cup, and I refilled it.

"Been meaning to ask you about a couple of things." The sheriff sipped his coffee. "We don't have your cell phone number. Do you mind giving it to me? And why don't you have a car? You have a valid driver's license. And yes, I know I'm prying into your personal business. It's my job, and besides that, my wife told me to." The sheriff grinned.

"I hadn't gotten around to getting a cell. I'll do it today. I'm nervous about driving after being out of practice for so long, but I guess a car might be handy."

"Give the dispatcher a call with your cell phone number. Gotta get to work. Glad I got that last donut." His radio crackled, and he hurried out.

I flipped my hand-painted Donut Hole sign from *Open* to *Closed! See You in the Morning*. The next few hours, I cleaned machines and prepared the shop for the next day. I frowned at the window after I tossed my apron into the hamper. *My visitor wasn't dressed like a child who lives with family.*

"Ready to go, Colonel? What would we do if one of our thunderstorms rolled through when we were ready to come to the work one morning? Let's visit our new sales manager and get a car. We'll get a cell phone too. Max can help with that."

Chapter Four

Colonel and I strolled to the car dealership. "I'm going to get fat if we get a car. You know that, don't you? I should have told the sheriff I didn't want to get fat."

When Colonel and I opened the door to the dealership, Dustin rushed to meet us. "Ms. Donut Lady, it's nice to see you." He grabbed my hand and shook it. "What can we do for you?"

"Colonel and I are here for a car."

"You'll need a four-door. Were you thinking new or gently used? Let's sit." He led me to a group of three comfortable chairs around a small round table.

"Gently used sounds like my style."

"I've got one in mind. Is it okay if I hand you off to one of our new salespeople? She started last week and could use the commission."

"That's fine."

"I'll get her, then we'll show you the car."

He returned with a tall twenty-year-old girl with red hair and tattoos on her arms.

"Ms. Donut Lady, this is Peyton. Peyton and I will show you a car we think you'll like."

"Hello, Ms. Donut Lady." Peyton offered her hand, and we shook.

"I know this car," Peyton said. "A young couple with two children turned it in for a larger one because they learned they have twins on the way. The youngest child spilled a red drink so there's a stain on the back seat, but the car's in good condition because they kept up the maintenance. Let's go look at it."

The four of us strolled to the car lot, and Peyton pointed to a silver car. "Looks new, doesn't it? Would you like to drive it?"

She opened the back door for Colonel, and he jumped inside. She opened the driver's door for me then walked around to the passenger's side.

"How long has it been since you've driven?" she asked.

"Quite a while. How did you know?"

"You aren't comfortable at all. We'll work on that. Raise the seat a little bit until you can see the back window in your rearview mirror. The control is on your lower left."

I reached down and pulled up on the button, and my seat rose. "That helped."

"Now stretch your right foot out and push the button to move you forward. Keep going forward until the ball of your foot touches the gas pedal." She bent over to watch my progress. "That's good. Press on the brake. How does that feel?"

"Natural. Comfortable."

"Is the angle of the seat okay? Maybe make the back a little straighter. That's the other control on the left lower side toward the back."

I shifted the seat to a more upright position. "This is better."

I checked my side mirrors and found the windshield wiper controls, headlights, and the levers to open the trunk and the fuel tank door.

"Ready to drive?" Peyton asked.

I turned the key and eased through the parking lot to the road. When I checked for cars, I glanced at Peyton. She was leaned back in her seat, and her hands were in her lap and relaxed. I frowned at my white knuckles and my hands that clenched the steering wheel. I wiggled my fingers and shook my hands then turned right and accelerated down the road.

I grinned. *More freedom.* I slowed and pulled into the gas station to turn around.

"What do you think so far?" Peyton asked.

"It's smooth. I like it."

When we returned, we opened the hood and Peyton showed me what to look for and what I could take care of myself. We found the spare tire and jack in the trunk.

"Ms. Donut Lady, buy a heavier duty jack and a good set of jumper cables. Don't change a tire yourself, but whoever changes a tire for you will appreciate a good jack. As far as the jumper cables, learn how to use them so you will know if they are being attached correctly. If they aren't, stop them and do it yourself."

We walked into the sales office where the sales manager waited for us. After he handed paperwork to Peyton, she and I sat at the round table, and she explained each page to me. After we completed our transaction, Peyton and I hugged, and Dustin beamed.

Colonel and I strolled out to my new car. "Let's go, boy. Cell phone next."

On our way to the computer store, I said, "Did I make a mistake? Should I have bought the cell phone first? I didn't think about parking. Should I take the car home then walk to town?"

I glanced in the back seat, and Colonel was asleep.

The parking in front of the computer store was parallel parking, but there were no cars close. I exhaled and pulled in between the white lines. When I got out of the car to let Colonel out, I realized I was three feet away from the front line and half in the other parking spot in the back. I climbed in and eased forward. *I'll need to work on that.*

Colonel took his position at the door. When I went inside, Max grinned. "Nice ride. What can I do for you?"

"I need a cell phone and have no idea what kind."

He smacked his forehead. "I should have thought about that when you got your laptop. You'll need to text and check the internet. We've got a couple different choices."

I followed him to a wall of cell phones. Max pointed to one. "I recommend this one. It's on sale and has all the features you'll need. It has good ratings, and the battery life is excellent."

He handed me the phone, and I stared at it.

"You'll be a pro in a week, but anytime you have any problems, questions, or excess donuts, come see me." Max guffawed, and I giggled.

He wiped his eyes. "I crack me up. Let's pick out a cover for you. Do you think you'll be hard on your phone?" He squinted at me and grinned. "Yep. You're a tough lady."

He turned to a display. "This case fits your phone. We've got a choice of covers. Here's black. That's popular. And silver."

He frowned at the covers. "I'd forgotten about this pink one. I need to take it down. They sent it to me by mistake and didn't want it returned."

He held out the black and silver cases. "Which one?"

"Pink."

His eyes widened. "Are you serious? If you'll take the pink one off my hands, I'll take a pink-sprinkled donut in exchange."

"Deal," I smiled, and we shook hands.

"Let's activate your phone, and I'll put the case on for you," he said.

When I walked out of the store, Colonel danced as he headed to our gently used car.

The next morning, I woke an hour earlier than usual. I sat up in bed, my heart pounding and my hair plastered on my damp forehead. Shadows fluttered in the hallway. *The Terry nightmare. Again.*

I swung my feet over the side of the bed and shuddered at the memory.

His body slammed onto my car hood, and his face hit the windshield. When his blood smeared across the glass, his demonic grin was even more horrifying.

I stumbled to the bathroom and splashed cold water on my face. The hairs on the back of my neck were prickly and heightened the lingering sense of unease and foreboding as I dressed.

When I stepped outside and saw how dense the fog was, I shuddered. *I can't drive in this.*

I went back into the house and grabbed my flashlight. After I stumbled a few yards in the reflected light, I gave up and switched off the light. *I'll rely on Colonel.* He stayed close while I touched his back with my fingertips for balance. Sounds were muffled and amplified at the same time. The dichotomy added to the sense of the unreal, and the familiar surroundings took on a spooky eeriness. Maybe I couldn't see around me, but nobody could see me either. *Is the boy wandering in the fog?*

He was still on my mind when I cut lard into the flour for tortillas at the shop. He reminded me of a new inmate, ready to bolt at the first hint of danger.

I didn't realize how tense I was until the boy appeared at the shop. I bit my lip. He wore the same clothes. I unlocked the door. "Good morning, more barter?"

He nodded. His left eye was black and swollen, and the knuckles on his right hand were scraped.

I put ice inside a plastic bag and wrapped the bag with a small towel. When I offered him the ice pack, he looked at the floor. I placed it on the counter.

"Same barter? Sweep for breakfast? I need a lot more help. What do you need? What else can we barter?"

"Sweep for breakfast like yesterday," he said. His face and voice were tight. When Colonel nudged his hand, I watched his face soften.

"You sweep. I'll get our breakfast ready."

I put the fresh dough in the tortilla press. My first tortilla was too thick, and it wouldn't fold, so I tried again. After the boy swept, he washed his hands.

"I may expand the morning menu to include eggs." I stood at the grill, browned a tortilla, and scrambled eggs. "Thought I'd make breakfast tacos. I'd like for you to try one and let me know what you think. Pick out your two donuts, and we can sit down."

I watched the boy stoop down and stroke Mia's back. She waved her tail and purred.

"You pick, okay?" he asked.

"Today's special is blueberry. How about a blueberry donut and a chocolate?"

"Yes, Miss."

He perched on a stool at the counter, and Colonel flopped at the boy's feet. I cut the breakfast taco into two equal portions and sat next to him.

He folded his hands. "Bless this food."

"And bless us. Oh, yum. I love warm donuts. Breakfast taco isn't bad either."

"Mmmm." He took a big swig of milk.

"You get into a fight?" I sipped my coffee.

He froze and stared at his plate. *He didn't run. Good first step.*

"Go ahead and put that ice on your eye. I need help in the afternoons." I munched and swallowed. "Maybe do one or two things a day. Like with the stockroom, you could put supplies on the shelves. Take Colonel for a walk or empty Mia's litter box. What do you need?"

The boy took in a big breath, held it, and let it out. Colonel and Mia watched him. I imagined they felt the same anticipation as me.

He held the ice pack on his eye. "They say you're a teacher. Are you?"

"I am. Well, I'm retired. But I was a teacher for a lot of years."

He lowered the ice pack and squinted his dark brown eyes at me. He had all the makings of an expert interrogator. "Were you a good teacher?"

"Yes, I was the best." And I was too. I was proud of the more than one hundred women I had taught to read. I was *Teach*.

He jumped off his stool and carried his plate and glass to the sink. "You good enough to teach me to read?"

"I certainly am. Ready to barter?"

"Maybe."

I stacked my cup on my plate and brushed the crumbs off the counter with my napkin onto my plate. "My name is Karen. What's yours?"

"They call me Haywood." He looked at Colonel. "My daddy called me Woody."

"Okay if I call you Woody?"

He nodded. *I'd reached a new status.*

Mia moved onto Woody's lap. He stroked her neck while he rubbed Colonel's face. "They used to call you the Lady Who Bought the Donut Shop. Now they call you the Donut Lady."

"A lot of people used to call me Teach, but I think I'm the Donut Lady."

"Miss Teach." He wrinkled his nose. "No. Miss Lady."

He rushed to the door but paused. "See you this afternoon." His voice was so quiet, it sounded like a voice in my head. *Is that what you meant, Shorty?*

He ran out the door and past the window.

"I'll be ready." I smiled.

Customers streamed into the shop all morning. The book club woman came in and offered her hand. As we shook hands, she said, "I'm Amber. I'm the mayor's daughter. Not trying to name-drop, but if I get into a fight, you'll know it's politics." She laughed, and I joined her.

I like Amber.

She sat at the counter and sipped her coffee while I waited on customers. "You could charge a modest sum for meetings and book clubs. Maybe by the hour. Just an idea. Might want to talk to the county health department and the city zoning people to see if it's feasible."

"That makes sense. I don't use the office. I like having my computer in the storeroom. It's cozy. Want to see what you think?" When I opened the office door, my eyes widened. "I forgot how large this room is. Smells musty. Look at the dust." I swiped my fingers across the top of the buffet. "This is embarrassing. I need your cleaning people."

Amber looked around. "You have a lot of room in here. Seems like you could set it up for a group. How big is that table in the corner?"

I tugged the table away from the wall. "This table's heavier than I thought."

Amber helped me move it to the middle of the room. "This would work. Just add folding chairs."

"Where do clubs meet in town now?" I asked.

"The library has meeting rooms, but they aren't available because the large organizations book them for their monthly meetings years in advance. The restaurants are available for parties, but we're not interested in meals; a small group more interested in discussion than eating really has nowhere to meet."

The bell jingled to announce another customer. The first customer held the door for the woman who followed her, and both of them left with donuts and scones.

"I can check with the health department and zoning for you, at least to see if it's possible," Amber said after the shop cleared. "Would that be okay?"

"Thank you. It'd be helpful to know if it's an option before I get too deep into planning."

As soon as I sold the last donut, I locked the door, flipped the sign, and hurried to the library for books for the afternoon. Colonel trotted along and waited outside to greet the library patrons. The library doors whooshed open, and I stepped inside.

A woman to my left sniffed, slammed a book with a thud on the table, and stormed out. My spirits plummeted. *What did I expect? It's a small town. Everybody knows I was in prison.* I trudged into the library.

"Ignore her. Her panties are in a wad today." The librarian waved her silver pen like a wand, and her metallic bracelets clinked.

I shook off the cloud of rejection. *Most forgive and forget. Some don't. Deal with it.*

The librarian wore a crimson shirt with a bright-yellow scarf double-draped around her neck. Her short, coal-black hair complemented her dangly turquoise and silver earrings that jingled when she moved her head. I liked her style.

"Looking for something special?"

"I need Easy Reader books for a ten-year-old boy."

I told her what I had in mind, and she tiptoed to the shelves, her steps accompanied by the jangles and clangs of her jewelry. She carried her pen in her palm. I wondered if a bewildered toad sat outside the library, and I hoped to see her pen in action again.

She pulled books off the shelf and thumbed through them. "I almost feel like plopping down and reading these myself."

I waggled my eyebrows. "We'd have to sit on the floor."

"Well, you first. I want to see you get back up, girlfriend." She shushed me when I giggled, and we silent-laughed with exaggerated shaking shoulders.

"I've got some data I need to analyze. It might help to talk it out with someone. Does that sound interesting to you?"

"Right up my alley. Come by any afternoon after you close the Donut Shop. I've got volunteers galore that would love to pilot this ship for a while."

After the library, I stopped at the grocery store for drinks, cheese, crackers, fruit, and yogurt for lunch and snacks. Colonel waited outside.

An elderly woman, another one of my frequent customers, stood at the cheese case with her hand-carved cane propped in her cart. She placed a package of sharp cheese in her basket and smiled as she patted her cane. "My late husband carved this for me. It's maple wood. I might have told you that before. I suppose you know Colonel's at the entrance with his fan club. He's very popular with my set, you know. Some of us aren't very social, but Colonel likes us anyway. But I'd come to your shop for your donuts even if Colonel wasn't there. I don't care what the others say."

I returned her smile. "Thank you."

I worked on a list of barter tasks at lunch. The opportunity to teach Woody to read brought a smile to my heart.

Woody ran up to the front door of the shop at the same time the afternoon shower began. "Beat it." He beamed.

I beamed too. *What a contrast to his scowl.*

While we sat at the counter and snacked on cheese and crackers, I handed him the barter list. He glanced at it. "Can you read it to me, Miss?"

After I read the list, he flexed his arms. "I'm good at lifting things. I'm stronger than I look."

"The storeroom is probably where I need help the most. I'll show you the sketch for organizing supplies on the shelves."

He pointed to a top shelf in my sketch. "You have heavy stuff on the low shelves, except what was this again?"

"Cooking oil. You're right, it belongs on a lower shelf. Good catch." I drew an arrow pointing to a lower shelf.

"Can we look?" he asked.

Woody touched each shelf in the storeroom and repeated the items that went on the shelf. "I can do this, Miss. I can remember good."

After an hour, I stuck my head into the storeroom. "That was fast. You've already shelved everything."

He grinned and pointed at the flattened empty boxes. "Where do these go, Miss?"

"The recycle bin is out back. We'll read after you come back inside."

We settled down in the corner where I'd moved two folding chairs. I held my book bag on my lap. "Before we start, did anyone ever read to you? When you were little?"

"Grandmama read some Bible to me, but her eyes were bad, so she mostly just told me Bible stories. Grandpappy read a book at bedtime about the moon. But they died when I was five."

"I know you miss them. I bet they'd be happy you want to learn to read."

Mia jumped onto Woody's lap. He stroked her back and nodded.

"I have another question," I said. "Did the school test you to see why you can't read?"

"Oh no, Miss. I skip school at test time. Everybody knows about testing. You have to sit still. They just held me back after that." He grinned.

And nobody questioned why or complained? "Well, that answers that. How about if I read to you to start?"

I pulled a graphic novel out of my book bag.

"But Miss Lady, that's not like a reading book. That's like a comic book."

"I know. Cool, right?"

Woody cocked his head to the side and raised an eyebrow. "You sure this here comic book counts as real reading?"

"Positive." I smiled at the suspicious tone and question I'd heard so many times in prison: *if it's fun, it can't be real learning, can it?*

We pushed our chairs together so both of us could see the pages, and I read. I allowed time for the story and pictures to soak in before I turned a page.

After a dozen pages, he gazed at the floor. "This story's about me."

"Why is that?" I had to strain to hear him.

"Because I get into trouble all the time too."

"Well, let's see how Geoff gets out of this one."

After an hour, I stretched my back. "We can stop here at the end of a chapter. We'll start with the next chapter tomorrow and finish the book. Okay?"

"Can we read one more page?"

I couldn't believe it. *I've waited my whole life to hear a child ask me to read one more page.*

"Of course. We'll finish the book, then you can feed Mia and take Colonel for a walk. How's that?"

"Yes, Miss."

Before Woody left, he lingered at the door. "How much would a banana cost me?

I raised my eyebrows. "You can have a banana any time. Free. It's included in your sweeping barter."

He stared at the floor and shifted his feet. "What about two?"

"No limit." I bit my lip to keep from asking why.

He dashed to the kitchen counter and picked up two bananas then hurried away.

Colonel stared at me.

"I have no idea what that was all about, but it certainly seemed important. He'll tell us later."

I locked up and strolled home as Colonel trotted ahead of me then returned with a grin.

I scrubbed a potato, placed it into the oven to bake, and created a spreadsheet of the addresses, buildings, and dates. I printed two copies of my spreadsheet then stared at the dates.

"What if the dates are for events? Maybe event one occurred on the first date and the last event occurred on the second date. We don't know how many events there were between the first and the last."

Colonel leaned against me, and shadows billowed in the hallway.

After Woody swept the next morning, I served our plates and drinks. While Woody ate his third donut, I sipped my coffee. "You having trouble in school?"

"No, Miss."

I raised my eyebrow. "I asked the wrong question. What kind of trouble you having in school?"

"People make fun of me because I can't read. I don't care." He jumped down from his stool and kicked it. The stool crashed to the floor, and Mia dashed to the storeroom. Colonel trotted to Woody and leaned against him.

He glared and clenched his fists, and his nostrils flared with his rapid breathing.

"They're jerks," I said.

He stomped out and slammed the door.

"It's a start, Colonel." I cleared the dishes and cleaned the counter.

As I righted the stool, the Sheriff strode in. "I just saw Woody running to school. Everything okay?"

"Sure is." I poured his coffee and set his plate of donuts on the counter.

He narrowed his eyes. "Will I hear the story later?"

I shrugged. "Probably."

He sipped his coffee. "I can't imagine facing my workday without first being fortified by this coffee and the best donuts on the planet. I've got a batch of new recruits starting today. I'd like two or three dozen donuts to get their careers off on the right path." He peered over his cup and waggled his eyebrows.

I stared. "Oh, I get it." I giggled, and he guffawed. "That was excellent, Sheriff. I needed a good laugh. I'll box up the donuts for you. They're on the house."

"Nope. Can't have you going out of business. Who else could I harass first thing in the morning?"

—ele—

The next morning, Woody was late. He came into the shop with a scowl. He grabbed the broom and swept at a furious pace that matched his mood. When he finished, he jammed the broom into the closet, and stomped to the counter.

"You ready for milk and your donuts?" I asked.

"I guess," he mumbled.

When I placed the maple and glazed donuts and glass of milk in front of him, he avoided my gaze and chomped down his donuts. After he gulped down his milk, he stormed to the front door. "I hate school. I'm not going today." The windows rattled from the force of the slammed door.

"What do you think, Colonel? Test day?"

—ele—

The next morning, Woody appeared in the window at his usual time. I waved, and he came into the shop. He remained in the doorway with the door open. His gray shirt was stained and torn, and his jeans were dirty at the knees and stained at the thighs where he'd wiped his hands. "Can I sweep for a donut and milk?".

"Certainly. Come on in." I continued frying donuts.

Woody swept with care, put away his broom, and stood in the middle of the room. He shifted his feet and stared at the floor. He spoke, but it was too low for me to hear.

I set his plate with a pink-sprinkled donut and a chocolate donut on the counter and turned to pour his milk.

"What did you say? I didn't hear you."

"Are you mad?"

"Of course not. Why would I be? Your donuts and milk are at your place." I poured a cup of coffee and plated my pink-sprinkled donut.

"I didn't go to school yesterday." He climbed up on the stool. "Bless this food and bless us."

"Amen." I joined him at the counter and took a bite. "Mmm, good. It must have been test day."

"Are you mad?"

"No. You told me you couldn't sit still for the tests. There's no reason for me to be mad. Maybe before the next test we can come up with some ideas to make it easier for you to take a test. Has a doctor checked you to see why you can't sit still?"

Woody stared at me. "Never been to a doctor. I don't get sick."

He finished his breakfast, picked up his backpack, and waved from the window.

The bell jingled, and the sheriff strode in. I poured coffee, plated his donuts, and sat at the counter.

"From the look on your face, I'd like to drink my coffee first," he said.

"Fine. Hurry up." I sipped my coffee.

The sheriff took a small bite of a chocolate donut, then set it on his plate. After he chewed his bite with deliberate care, he took a small sip of coffee and grinned.

I drank my coffee and rose. I waved the coffee pot. "I'm getting a refill. What about you?"

"Not fair. You cheat." He drained his cup, and I refilled both our cups.

"I asked Woody if the doctor checked him to see why he couldn't sit still long enough to take a test. Did you know he has never been to a doctor?"

"You're kidding. The county pays for medical care and medications. I'll look into that. I'd say maybe Woody's mistaken, but my gut believes him."

"Mine too."

The following week, Woody finished his afternoon snack and leaned back in his chair. "We read three books last week. I'm ready to beat that record."

I smiled at the pride in his voice.

After he left for the day, I pursed my lips and pondered our reading corner. "Want to go for a ride, Colonel? Let's check the thrift store for reading chairs."

Colonel wagged his tail, picked up his leash with his teeth, and ran to the door with his don't-have-to-ask-me-twice look.

The owner, Giselle, greeted us at the door. She reminded me of one of my favorite officers at the prison. Tall and slender, with a broad grin that could coax a smile out of the most bitter inmate. She wore a sage green T-shirt with jeans and a white utility apron with handprints of dirt and dust. "Looking for anything special?"

"I need two comfortable reading chairs. And maybe a table, not too big."

She brushed her hands on her apron. "Are you sprucing up your shop?"

"Hadn't thought about it that way, but I guess I am."

"I might get some chairs next week. Meanwhile, what do you think of this round table? It's real wood. Needs work."

"Just what I had in mind."

We haggled over the price, and when we settled, my bonus was her grin. I don't know what was more fun: finding the table or negotiating the price.

"One more thing," Giselle said. "Do you like this floor lamp? I'll throw it in as a shop-warming gift."

"Are you sure? It's beautiful. Isn't that a leaded stained-glass shade?"

"Good eye. Yes, it is. I love that lamp; if I sold it, I'd never see it again, but if it's in your shop, I'll be able to enjoy it."

"It's a wonderful gift. Thank you very much."

Giselle carried the table, and I followed her with the floor lamp. After we loaded the furniture into my car, she placed her hand on my arm. "Thank you for your work with Haywood. I've been worried about him. Everybody knows how much better he's doing in school. My mother was related to his grandmother's side. He's family to me."

I smiled. "He's intelligent and interested in learning. He's been a joy to work with."

She headed toward the thrift store then stopped. She frowned as she turned. "You know those people he stays with are supposed to be relatives of his mother, but most of us think they aren't. His mother was fair-skinned. Those people don't look like her one bit."

Woody spotted the table when he arrived that afternoon. "Cool table. Can I refinish it?"

"That'd be great. Let's go to the hardware store after our snack and pick up what you need."

I strolled to the store. Woody hopped and skipped in front of me, and Colonel dashed back and forth between us. We returned with different grades of sandpaper, a finishing cloth, hand cleaner, and stain.

Chapter Five

On our way back I said, "Get into any trouble today?"

Woody jerked his head, stopped, and turned to look at me. I raised my eyebrows and smiled.

He laughed. "Not anything like Geoff."

I faked a sober look. "Good to know the principal's car isn't in a pool."

"You got me, Miss Lady." He held up his hand, and I smacked it in our usual high-five style.

Woody spent three afternoons on our little table. When he finished, he motioned at his handiwork. "What do you think?"

"That is beautiful, Woody. You transformed that old table into an expensive piece of furniture. Your grandpa teach you that?"

Woody's face lit up. "Yep. Grandpappy let me sand, even when the work was for his best customer. He said nobody sanded good and careful like me."

And he was just a little boy. What an awesome grandfather to encourage the child's talents.

After our reading session, I closed our latest book. "The end. Next week we'll read the first book together. How does that sound?"

"Good."

After we reread the first book, Woody read the second book with minimal prompts on words when he got stuck.

"I need to learn writin'. What would writin' cost me?"

"I'll throw it in for free. Like a bonus. I'll get you a notebook so you can practice."

After Woody left, I locked up the shop and hurried home to pick up my spreadsheets and laptop then rushed to the library. Monica, the librarian, grinned when I dashed in. She wore a deep purple blouse with ruffles on the sleeves and a hunter-orange triangular scarf tied at the back of her neck. Her scarf could double as protection against a sandstorm or as a bank robber's mask if she pulled it up over her nose. Her dangling earrings were tiny hatchets. *Monica is awesome.*

"Let me grab a volunteer and my laptop then we can work in one of the meeting rooms upstairs without being interrupted."

She retrieved her computer from her office and when she twirled her silver pen, her metallic bracelets jangled. A volunteer bustled to the checkout desk.

"I need someone to manage the desk for two hours," Monica said. "Is that something you would like to do?"

The volunteer beamed. "Yes, ma'am. You take your time, Ms. Monica."

Monica led the way to a corner meeting room on the second floor. The two walls of windows brought in the outside. "This is perfect. It's almost like working outside," I said.

"It helps when our brains aren't constricted by walls."

I gave her a copy of the spreadsheet. "This information was inside an envelope. A friend set the envelope on my book cart in the prison library then dropped a book on top of the envelope. It seemed deliberate. I hid the envelope and smuggled it out of the library. She may have planned to come back for it later, but she was murdered."

Monica studied the sheet. "What was her name?"

I raised my eyebrows. "Her prison name was Shorty."

"Did Shorty say anything?"

"Shorty heard voices nobody else heard. She said her voices said someone would sneak up behind her, and that's how she would die. I think she was right."

Monica tapped the spreadsheet with her silver pen. "What else? There's something else."

I gazed at the ceiling and replayed the conversation in my head. "She said she had a talent. She saw patterns in death. No. She said she saw patterns *of* death."

"Well, then. She made it easy for us. I'll take one address, and you take another one. We're looking for patterns of death, right?"

"That must be it. So, what we're looking for in this first one is patterns of death in Knoxville between the two dates. But how does the sheriff's office fit in?"

"We look for any patterns of death the sheriff's office investigated. Or maybe the sheriff's office was involved. You want to take Knoxville? I'll take the second one, Pittsburgh. I think we should move slowly, take our time, look for patterns."

After two hours, we took a break. "I found six deaths on hiking paths that occurred in the three years between our Knoxville dates. There were no deaths on the paths the two years before or the two years after. The sheriff's office led the investigation until the state stepped in after the last death. All the deaths were lone hikers who fell, and the medical examiners ruled all as accidental."

"Interesting. I bogged down in studies of murders in Pittsburgh with data by gender, race, relationship to killer, age, and even receipt of public assistance. It could have been data for any large city, and there was nothing special about the date boundaries."

She squinted at the ceiling. "When I broadened my search to the Pittsburgh area, I noticed several hiking trails not to mention some restaurants that sounded amazing and a definite region-wide obsession with football."

Monica rolled her eyes. "Easy to forget my original search. The hiking trails might be something to look into. Or the patterns of death might be different for each location. Maybe the overall pattern included under investigation by law enforcement and ruled accidental."

"Ready to give it a break for a few days?" I turned off my computer.

"That's a good idea. Fresh eyes and fresh minds." Monica rose. "Can I keep the spreadsheet?"

"You'll keep searching, won't you?" I snickered.

"If the mood strikes me." Monica grinned.

After Woody left the next morning, the sheriff slid onto his usual seat at the counter. "How's the reading program?"

I poured two cups of coffee. "Woody's a sponge. He's so thirsty to learn."

"His daddy was smart, but he got into trouble in school because he was so restless. Hyperactive, they said. The baseball coach worked with him, and his grades shot up. Sounds like Woody's like his dad. Just needs somebody who can work with him. Hmm. Might mention that to the School Resource Officer."

My face warmed, and I felt my blood pressure rise. "How does a boy fall through the cracks like that? Why didn't anyone notice? Or care?"

"Not up to you to get involved, Ms. Karen."

"Somebody needs to." My frustration boiled inside me. I stood up and paced, but it didn't help. "Have you heard the talk that the people he stays with aren't related to his mother?"

The sheriff's eyes narrowed. "They claimed they are. There were some special concessions and higher payments because they are relatives. Hadn't heard they aren't. Why don't I schedule a meeting with his caseworker? It may be awhile. She's stretched thin. But I can ask her to send me the documentation on the Dixons, including Woody's medical appointments."

I massaged my palms with my thumbs to soothe away the anxiety. "It's a place to start. Thanks."

How do we find any of his mother's relatives? I smiled. *I know who would know.*

The sheriff frowned. "Ms. Karen, I don't like it when you smile like that. Stay out of trouble. Ya hear?"

"Of course." I widened my eyes so I wouldn't do the smile he didn't like.

Shirley rushed into the shop not long after the sheriff left. "I need a donut and a scone this morning, Karen. I have to go to the regional meeting today. My partner is the main speaker, and she said I have to be there. When I told her it made more sense for me to be working, she got grumpy. Now I have to sit still and listen to talks all afternoon even though I told her she could take notes, and I'd read them. She got grumpier."

"Blueberry scones today."

"Blueberry sounds great. They are good for you, right? Some kind of anti-something. I need a dose of anti-something to survive the day and how about a classic? Got any left?"

"Yes." I put her pastries into a sack and poured her coffee. "I have a question. You said the Dixons aren't related to Woody's mother, right? Where are her relatives?"

She sat on a stool at the counter. "No, they aren't. I don't know where her relatives are. Kinsey had terminal cancer and died when Haywood was two. His grandparents took him in."

I dropped onto a stool. My voice squeaked. "Why didn't you tell me this before?"

"Everybody knew about Kinsey and how sick she was before she died. I guess I thought you did too. I don't like to think about it. She was a wonderful person and a good mother."

My stomach was in knots. "So why are you so negative about Woody?"

She jumped up and grabbed her coffee and sack. "I'm just so afraid. I guess I've always thought if I think the worst, nobody can ever disappoint me. Gotta go."

I still don't understand Shirley.

After I locked up at the end of my morning, a tapping sound caught my attention. I glanced up, and Woody peered through the window. When I unlocked the door, he came into the shop with his head down.

"I'm suspended until Monday." He mumbled then raised his head and gazed at me. His left eye was swollen and bruised, and he had an abrasion on his forehead. I glanced at his hands and his scraped knuckles.

"Let's clean you up and get some ice on that eye. Sit at the counter."

I returned with a bowl of warm water, a cloth, and an ice pack. While I cleaned his face, I asked, "What was the fight about?"

He scowled and turned his head away. "Nuthin'."

I waited. He glanced at me, and I raised my eyebrows.

"I'm not stupid." Colonel padded over to Woody and flopped down.

"You're right. You are actually quite intelligent. Were you suspended for fighting?"

"Yes, Miss."

"With other boys? How many?"

"Three." He removed the ice pack.

"Keep your ice on your eye. Would you like some crackers and cheese? A sandwich and milk?"

"Yes, Miss. I'm missing lunch at school."

While he ate, I asked, "Were the other boys suspended too?"

"Oh no, Miss. They never get suspended. I'm a troublemaker."

"Is that so? I'm going to your school to have a chat with the principal. Would you be okay to stay here and take care of Colonel and Mia for me? Or do you want to go with me?"

He bit his lip. "I guess I'll stay with Colonel and Mia."

I parked at the school and marched to the principal's office then tapped on his door and walked in. The principal was eating lunch at his desk. He looked up in surprise. "Do we have an appointment, Ms. O'Brien?" He frowned at his computer. "I see nothing on my calendar."

"No. No appointment. I'm here to talk to you about Haywood. I understand you suspended him for fighting." I sat in his visitor's chair and scooted closer to his desk.

"Yes. This morning. That one's trouble."

"Hmm. Is that so? What was the fight about? How many were involved?"

He straightened his back and leaned forward. "I don't see what business it is of yours."

I narrowed my eyes. "You know I'm Haywood's tutor. I'm required to report any injuries." I rose.

"Wait, wait. Let me look at his records." He turned to his computer. "Four boys involved. Hmm. Two of the boys are a year older than Haywood. Hmm. We suspended only Haywood? That's not our policy. I'm reversing the suspension…"

He scrolled his screen and frowned. "It looks like we have suspended Haywood several other times for fighting, and he was the only one suspended." He shook his head. "I'm investigating this. You'll tell Haywood he's not suspended? I'll talk to him when he comes to school tomorrow."

"I expect a full report. You can get in touch with me or the sheriff. Enjoy your lunch."

I closed his office door with care as I left even though my hands shook. *I sure wanted to slam that door.* After a few slow breaths, I relaxed.

When I returned to the shop, both Woody and Colonel were curled on the floor and asleep. The bell jingled, and Woody rubbed his eyes and sat up. "You get into any trouble at school today, Miss Lady?"

I smiled at the memory of the principal's face. "I think I got in a little trouble, but the principal said you aren't suspended. It'll take more than three bullies to keep you out of school."

———*elle*———

When the sheriff sauntered in the next morning, he sat at the counter. "I got a call from the principal yesterday afternoon. What did you do to scare him? He said he investigated Haywood's fights and discovered Haywood's been defending himself against three larger boys. He wanted me to know before you reported him. The school counselor requested meetings with all four sets of parents. She plans to help the parents find family counselors. What were you going to report him for?"

"I might have indicated I had an obligation to report injuries of a minor. I told him he could report his findings about Woody to me or to you." I jumped up and grabbed the coffee pot.

After I poured, the sheriff blew on his hot coffee. "You must have struck a nerve. From what he said, it sounds like the school stuck a label on Haywood and didn't check facts. Easy to do when no one's paying attention or advocating for a child, and the other parents have the potential to create a big stink."

"The advantage of being a retired teacher is I knew the right words."

"You've made a difference for Woody. You've got magic."

"Sometimes I wish I did."

The bell jingled, and the man from the dry cleaners came in. "Today's my birthday. My wife said it's good luck to give customers a treat on my birthday. I didn't know that, but after thirty-four years, I don't argue. I need four dozen donuts, and I apologize for not calling you when my wife told me to last week."

I smiled. "Four dozen coming right up." He met me at the cash register and paid me. He looked at his receipt.

"You made a mistake. You've charged me for three dozen. I wanted four."

"You have four. Happy birthday."

He beamed. "You are the best Donut Lady in town."

After he left, the sheriff chuckled. "Didn't know about the rest of the donut ladies."

"He was so sincere. I couldn't laugh at him, but it sure was hard to hold it in." I sipped my coffee.

The sheriff's radio crackled. "Gotta run."

That afternoon, Woody hopped down from his stool after our snacks, and I picked up our snack plates. "Woody, would you like to have some help with your homework?"

He looked toward the back of the store and shifted his feet. I got the impression the storeroom was a haven. "I'm good."

"The offer's always open. Just let me know."

Woody carried his milk to our reading corner and picked up our latest book. After he read the chapter, Woody drained his glass of milk. "What would homework cost me in barter?"

I was ready with the answer. "I need the front window cleaned inside and out every day."

"I can do that."

We shook hands. Deal.

The next morning, Amber rushed in not long after the Sheriff left. "Need a maple donut. Don't bother to put it in a sack. Oh, make it two. Put one in a sack and one in my hand. I talked to the zoning people and the health department. No problem for you. You'll just need to apply for their permits."

I handed Amber a donut and her sack. When she pulled out her wallet, I waved off her money. "On the house. Consider it your commission for the legwork."

She took a bite of her donut. "Let me know if you need me to do anything else. I do my best work for maple."

Later, the bell jingled, and my next customer surprised me. "Sheriff, is this a coffee emergency? I never see you a second time after your morning stop."

He grinned and held up a brown paper sack with a large piece of wood sticking out. "Got something for you and Haywood." He pulled a shelf out of the sack. "One of my deputies is handy at woodcrafts, and he used an old plank he had on hand. He thought Haywood would like a bookshelf."

"This is beautiful work. I love the swirls and the character of the wood." I stroked my fingers across its smooth surface. *Old bookshelf, you'll fit right in.*

"He went to school with Woody's dad. Let me know if you need any help with installing it."

My eyes misted. "Thank you. We appreciate it."

I cleaned the shop in record time. I called Mr. Otto's accountant and made an appointment to talk about renting the office as a meeting room. I still had the rest of the afternoon left, and all I thought about was the bookshelf. *Now, what do I do? I can't wait until Woody sees it.*

"Want to go for a walk, Colonel? I've got energy I need to burn."

Colonel trotted to the door. I power-walked around the block, and Colonel led the way. After one time around, I stopped to catch my breath. Colonel and I headed to the park at a pace less likely to give an old woman a heart attack.

Colonel found a small tree branch and brought it to me. I threw it, Colonel took off after a squirrel, and I jogged to the stick. Colonel ran to me and sat with his doggie grin and his tongue out.

"You fooling me, or you want to play?"

I tapped the branch on my hand, and he watched. I threw the stick, and Colonel stared at me, glanced in the wood's direction, and sprinted after another squirrel.

"Next time, I'll chase the squirrels," I said.

I limped to the closest park bench where I emptied a speck of gravel out of my shoe then leaned back and watched Colonel clear the grounds of squirrels. He flopped at my feet and panted hard.

"Let's get you a drink, boy." I filled the park dog bowl at the park's faucet. After he drank his fill, we sauntered back to the shop.

On the way back, my mind wandered to hiking. *Don't most people go hiking with a companion?*

Colonel and I stepped into the welcoming comfort of air conditioning. I heard a rattle near the reading table and froze. Rattlesnake? I listened, and the sound was more of a rustle. Colonel trotted to the corner. Mia peeked out of the paper sack.

I grabbed a napkin and fanned my face. *Bookshelf, cat toy, and anxiety attack; can't beat that for a full-circle present.*

After school let out, Colonel and I waited for Woody outside the shop. Colonel pranced when Woody appeared down the street. "I understand, boy. I'm excited too."

When Woody got to the shop, I grinned. "I have a surprise for you."

I'd left the shelf on the counter. "For me, Miss? It's mine? Where did it come from? Where do we put it?"

"A deputy sheriff who was your dad's friend in school made it for you. You decide."

He held the bookshelf in his hands and ran his fingertips across the wood with a light, almost reverent touch. "Wow. For me."

He scanned the shop, crossed the room with the shelf under his arm to our corner, and put his hand on the wall. "How about right here?"

I nodded. "Perfect. The deputy included screws to hang the shelf, and I have an electric screwdriver. Did you want to put it up? Or shall I?"

"Do we have a level?"

"Mr. Otto left a bucket of tools in the storeroom. Want to look there?"

Woody marched out of the storeroom and waved a level like a baton. I beamed at his silliness, stepped into line behind him, and we paraded around the shop and to our reading corner.

Woody tapped on the wall, located the studs, and made light pencil marks for placement of the shelf. I held the bookshelf in place while Woody checked it with the level. He corrected his marks and installed the screws.

I shook my head in awe of his skill. "Who taught you to use an electric screwdriver and a level?"

"Grandpappy. I held the level and watched him."

After Woody installed the bookshelf, we wrote a thank-you note. Woody dictated; I scribed. He sketched the bookshelf and our reading corner at the bottom of the note.

I stared at the page. "Wow, Woody. Your sketch is amazing in depth and detail. It's a perfect depiction of our reading spot."

He blushed. "Drawing is easy."

"What goes on your bookshelf?" I asked while we ate a celebratory snack of yogurt and grapes.

"Books I can read. It's my trophy shelf."

I nodded. "I have an idea. Why don't we get you a backpack for your homework?"

On our way to the store, I lagged behind Woody and Colonel. Woody skipped and ran, and Colonel trotted along next to him. They stood outside the store and waited for me. Woody inspected backpacks, and I noticed he checked the prices.

"Don't worry about the cost, Woody. I've got a backpack budget, and these are within my budget."

Woody picked out a superhero backpack, and we headed for the shop.

While we ate apple and cheese slices, Woody spun on his stool and pointed at our corner. "Can I leave my backpack here?" He furrowed his brow and bit his lip.

I nodded. "Good idea. It will be here in the mornings with your finished homework for you to take to school every day."

We toasted Woody's plan with apple slices. "Cheers."

After lunch the next day, I slid my laptop into my backpack, and Colonel and I headed to the library. On the way, a movement overhead caught my attention, and I stared at a hawk as it glided overhead in a search for lunch. "I love watching the silent hunter at…"

I stumbled over a crack in the sidewalk and grabbed at the nearby picket fence that kept me from falling.

"Ouch." I peered at my hand. My palm had an abrasion but wasn't bleeding. *No splinters.*

"I injured my pride, Colonel. You'd think I'd know walking and staring at the sky don't make the best combination for multitasking. I would have fallen if the fence hadn't been there."

Colonel padded along beside me the rest of the way to the library then waited outside while I went inside.

"Ah ha," Monica said. "You're just in time. I found something in Pittsburgh." She wore a flowing orange gauze dress with a bottle-green fringed shawl. One earring was a brown wooden acoustic guitar, and the other one was a silver electric guitar. She tapped her pen, and her metallic bracelets jangled.

"Desk duty?" A heavy-set woman with her walker zipped past me.

"I will be in a meeting for two hours or more." Monica whirled her pen.

"I've got you covered," the woman said.

Monica retrieved her laptop from her office. "You're in charge."

As we headed up the stairs, I glanced back at the desk. The woman pumped her fist and mouthed, "Yes."

I snickered.

When we went into the meeting room, Monica said, "I think she has desk duty radar. What have you got for me?"

"I stumbled on the sidewalk and almost fell on the way here, but it reminded me of what Shorty's friend, Twitch, told me. Shorty's voices said Twitch needed to know falling was dangerous. I'm wondering if the Knoxville falls are a coincidence."

"Might be. For people who believe in coincidences. I don't. What else do you have?"

I stared at Monica. "Just a thought...don't most hikers have a companion? I've never been hiking. I don't know. And for some reason, *desk duty radar* reminded me of something, but I'm not sure what."

"You'll think of it when you're not thinking of it," Monica said. "Speaking of stumbling, we may have found more falls. I found twelve cases of deaths because of falls on hiking trails around Pittsburgh all within the five years listed for Pittsburgh. No fatal falls in the two years prior to our early date or two years after the latest date. Before we break into a victory dance, let's check two more. Number three on our list is Yakima, Washington, and number four is Albuquerque, New Mexico. You take Yakima, and I'll take Albuquerque, and let's look for falls."

I checked the dates for Yakima. "Three years, and the start date is almost a year after the end date of Pittsburgh. There was six months between the end of Knoxville and Pittsburgh."

"You're on to something there. Assuming our falls are murders, does our killer relocate to a new place and take a little time to get acquainted with the new trails?" Monica asked.

"So we're tracking a serial killer?" My eyes widened.

"Only in our minds." Monica chuckled.

After two hours, Monica stretched. "There are a bunch of places to climb and fall from around Albuquerque."

I rose and stared out the window. "Same thing with Yakima. There are more people getting lost on hikes than there are falls. Wonder if some of those lost but not found hikers fell?"

"Muddies it up because I'll bet some people who were lost weren't always reported when they were found."

"We're at the mercy of whether someone decides a person lost for a few hours is interesting enough to report," I grumbled.

"After we get our list of people who fell and died, maybe we go back to law enforcement for public information requests for the investigations," Monica said.

"Each state probably has a different process, but it gives us a better source."

"We've gotten farther than I would have if I tried to do this myself."

"I'm enjoying the thrill of the hunt. Thanks for bringing me in." Monica rose. "Time to go see if there was any drama downstairs, and answer the more important question, do we even care?" Monica laughed, and I joined her.

After I spent all Sunday afternoon on the computer, I rose to pour a glass of sweet tea and sat on the back porch. While Colonel patrolled for squirrels, I stared at my spreadsheet of hikers who fell or were lost in the Yakima area.

"According to my spreadsheet, the number one hobby in Yakima is falling and getting lost. Wonder if Monica's finding the same thing in Albuquerque?"

When I went inside the house to read, I glanced at the computer. "Is the age of the person who fell significant?"

After I fed Colonel, I spent the rest of the evening on the computer. I stopped at nine to throw together a cheese sandwich. After I'd eaten half my sandwich, I poured a glass of sweet tea and gulped down half of it.

"Cheese and bread by themselves are dry. Remind me to add a little mayonnaise and mustard next time, Colonel."

I finished my dry sandwich and gazed at my results. *Dead end.*

"Wouldn't you think most of the hikers were young, Colonel? Lots of people my age hike. Now I feel bad."

―― ele ――

Monday afternoon, Woody stood in the shop doorway with a big grin. "Get into any trouble today?"

I looked at Colonel and wondered if all the times I tuned out Shirley counted.

"Not anything like Geoff." I waited for the punch line.

"Me neither, and I've got my report card." Woody scrunched his shoulders. His eyes twinkled as he grinned.

First time he's ever mentioned a report card.

I laughed. "Really? You got me this time."

He handed me a manila envelope, and my hands shook in my excitement.

I sat on the nearest stool. "Look how much you've improved. Look at this, up to a C plus in reading and a C in math. All your grades came up. Awesome! And here's a note: 'Greatly improved' with two exclamation marks. And underlined. This is wonderful."

Woody shifted from foot to foot and grinned then sneezed.

I flipped the card over. "Bless you. Did you see this side? The learning skills category? Your teacher marked every single one of them *Satisfactory*. No, wait. She marked Responsibility *Excellent*. Congratulations, Woody."

The excitement in my voice caught Colonel and Mia's attention. Colonel threw back his head and howled, and Mia rubbed against my legs and purred.

"How about a new book to celebrate?" I asked. "We'll go to the bookstore, and you can pick."

He looked at me with an even bigger grin on his flushed face. "Yes, Miss."

Colonel trotted to the door and nudged it.

"Guess Colonel wants to go along. I'll get his leash," I said.

I locked the shop then we headed downtown. I carried Colonel's leash to look respectable. On the way to the bookstore, I asked, "What kind of book are you going to get? The next book in the series?"

"Another graphic novel. Maybe something new. No. More Geoff. How many more Geoff books are there? How many more report cards do I get this year? Do I get a new book every report card? It's great to read. Why was it such a big secret?"

"If you and Colonel want to run ahead, I'll be right behind you."

Woody and Colonel took off.

I snickered. *Maybe far behind you.*

When I reached the bookstore, Colonel was in his sentry position outside the door, and Woody and the young clerk were on the floor with six books spread in front of them and four books stacked next to the clerk.

"I picked books I might like, and we're putting them in TBR order. Miss Cathy said that means *to be read.*" Woody beamed.

Woody handed Cathy a book, and she recorded it then added it to the stack. "I'll keep Woody's list here so he can check it when he's ready for his next book."

"That's the smartest thing I ever heard." I sat in a nearby overstuffed chair and listened to Woody's excited chatter. Woody and Cathy carried the books to the register. Woody shifted the order of three books, and Cathy adjusted his reading list. After she and Woody verified the order of the books, she printed his name at the top of the page.

"Sign your list, Woody, so we know it's official," she said.

"Do you want me to put the books back on the shelves?" he asked.

"Or you could carry them for me, and I'll put them away. Your choice."

"They're heavy. I'll carry them." He picked up the stack of books and followed her to the shelves where they belonged then he sneezed.

"Bless you," Cathy said. "You coming down with a cold?"

"Don't think so. Sometimes I sneeze after I run, and Colonel and I raced here."

"Let's get you checked out. Are you going to read your new book today?"

Woody peered at me, and I said, "Your choice."

"Yes, I am," he said with pride in his voice.

On our way back to the shop, Woody hummed as he skipped with his book under his arm.

As I unlocked the shop door, I asked, "Snack?"

"Yes, Miss. I'll help." He sniffled then rushed to the cabinet and pulled out two plates and filled two glasses with water.

I cut an apple in half and sliced the sharp cheddar cheese we liked. After we ate our snack, I put our dishes in the dishwasher.

We scooted the two chairs together, and Woody read to me.

"I think this is the best of Geoff's books so far."

"Yes, Miss. Five stars." He added his book to his stack. "I'll see you in the morning."

"Thanks for reading to me. Have a good night."

Woody bounced out of the shop, and after I locked the door, Colonel and I headed home.

"I feel like bouncing too. What a great day, Colonel."

When the sheriff came in the next morning, I sprang to pour his coffee.

"You're looking chipper this morning. What's up?" he asked.

I served his coffee and donuts and sat at the counter next to him. I sipped my coffee. "Woody brought home, I mean the shop, a stellar report card yesterday. The lowest grade was a C. He was so proud, and so was I. His teacher marked all of his learning skills *Satisfactory* except *Responsibility* which she marked Excellent. We went to the bookstore for his reward."

The sheriff chuckled. "Not many kids think a book is a reward." The sheriff sneezed. "He's a special kid."

"Bless you. Something must be going around. Woody's sneezing too."

"Mine are allergies. I can deal with just about anything except changing weather."

I refilled our coffee. "What? Isn't that what our weather does?"

He nodded. "Pretty much." His radio crackled, and I dashed to sack up two donuts then he hurried to his cruiser with his sack in his hand.

After my last customer left, I called Monica and left a message. "It's Karen. Yakima has a history of falls and lost hikers, but it's constant. I will check Boulder, Colorado."

I sanitized the counter and the display case then put away the dried pots and pans from the dishwasher. When I passed the freezer, I remembered the frozen donuts.

"Let's take donuts to the Soup Kitchen, Colonel."

Colonel opened one eye then went back to sleep.

"Okay, lazy dog. I'll go by myself."

I loaded the ten dozen donuts into my car and drove to the soup kitchen. When I stepped inside, the same elderly woman as the first time I visited the soup kitchen peeked into the lobby and disappeared.

Now what? Carry in boxes?

Melinda Wallace rushed out of the kitchen. "Hey there, Donut Lady. You here for a hand out?" She cackled, and I grinned.

"Pretty close to it. I have ten dozen frozen donuts in my car I need to hand off to you. Want to give me a hand in carrying them inside?"

"Well said. I'd love to."

Melinda and I strolled to my car.

"I haven't been outside since early this morning," she said. "Listen to that bird sing. What a beautiful day."

I stopped. The blue sky was clear, the slight breeze from the south promised a warmer afternoon, and a mockingbird sang through its repertoire.

"It certainly is. Thanks for the reminder."

As we unloaded the donuts, I said, "You can thaw what you want to serve tomorrow and keep the rest frozen for later."

Melinda balanced the five dozen she carried and opened the door. "That works. Five dozen is perfect for one day."

I set my five dozen on the counter while she put hers in the freezer.

"Thanks again." Melinda moved the five dozen I'd brought in to the refrigerator. "This is a very generous donation. Our bookkeeper will send you a receipt for your records. Are the biddies getting you down?"

"Nope. How about you?"

"Same." She hugged me, and I left to pick up Colonel.

As I arrived at the shop, Monica called me. "I'm on my way to another meeting, but Albuquerque was similar to what you found in Yakima. I'll move on to Albany, New York when I get a chance. Later."

Chapter Six

When I opened the shop door, Mia was in her carrier, and Colonel dashed to the car. After we got home, I ate my yogurt and sat at my computer. Three hours later, I leaned back and stared at my screen.

I called Monica. "I think our killer got smarter and moved to places where the homicides hid in the group of accidental deaths."

"You may be right, girlfriend. So far, Albany's looking the same way. Now what?"

"I need to think."

"Right there with you."

When Woody came in Thursday morning, he had a cough in addition to the sniffles from earlier in the week, and his face was flushed.

He sneezed into the crook of his elbow as he washed his hands. "I should stay away from the food with this a bad cold."

"Would you care for some tea and honey? Maybe that will help your cough."

Woody nodded and dropped on his chair at our reading table. "Okay if I eat here?"

"Good idea. We'll isolate your germs. I'll scrub the table after you leave."

"Thank you. I was afraid I shouldn't come inside."

"Why don't you take a sick day and skip sweeping until you get better?"

"Thank you, Miss." He sank onto his chair, and I placed his hot cup of tea on the table in front of him. When he picked up the cup, he held it with two hands and sipped. "I like tea with honey. I didn't know that. My scratchy throat feels better."

Friday morning, Woody stopped to cough at the shop door before he came inside. His eyes were watering, and his face was flush.

"Is everything okay?" I asked.

"I think my cold is worse." His voice was raspy. "Can I have hot tea and honey again?" He cleared his throat then coughed. His cough sounded deep and wet.

"Of course. You're not sounding so great. Did you see the doctor?" I made his tea and set it on the counter.

He sipped the tea between labored breaths. "The lady said if I wasn't better by Monday, she'd take me to the doctor."

I furrowed my brow. "Do you want to stay here and not go to school today?"

"No, I better go to school. The lady told me if I miss one more day of school this year, I can't go back." He was overcome with a coughing spell. "School is important."

I worried about Woody the rest of the morning. After I cleaned the shop and was ready to leave, Giselle called from the thrift store.

"Donut Lady, I found two chairs that'll be perfect for your reading nook. Don't match, not the latest style, but they're clean and comfortable. Come see what you think."

Colonel and I hurried to her shop. I breathed in the light vanilla fragrance that greeted us at the door. Giselle's store didn't have the jumbled look of most thrift and antique shops; instead, she had arranged the gently used furniture into beckoning areas of relaxation. I paused to enjoy the welcoming reception as it wrapped around me.

I broke away from my reverie and spotted the chairs. I plopped down from one to the other to check them. "You're right. They're comfortable." *The total mismatch in pattern and color adds to their charm. Time to haggle.*

I rose and crossed my arms. "But style? Is this the best you could do? I walked all the way over here for these? Well, I'll give you five dollars for both and take them off your hands." I used my best trash-talk tone.

She lifted her chin, and I caught the gleam in her eye. "I need to call the sheriff. I got highway robbery in progress. I'll take pity on you and take thirty dollars each, and, since I'm such a nice person, a dozen free donuts every week."

I rubbed my face to hide my grin. *Love a challenge.* I strolled around the chairs twice and picked an imaginary thread off one. "Hmmph. Falling apart. Downright dangerous. How about fifteen dollars for the two of them and one free donut on your birthday?"

She crossed her arms and snorted. "You give everybody a free donut on their birthday. I'll take twenty dollars for the two and knock that back to a half-dozen donuts every Monday."

"You want to put me out of business? Okay on the twenty for two. I can go three donuts every other week."

"I'll suffer with three donuts every Monday."

I was ready for her. "One."

Giselle rolled her eyes, looked at the ceiling, and threw her hands up. For a minute, I thought she planned to bring lightning down on me. She was the best I'd ever haggled with, and I'd done a lot of haggling. Reading lessons were a high-value commodity in prison.

"Do you a favor. Two, and we're good."

I'm not near as good as you are, though. Wait, got an idea.

"Okay, you got it. Two free donuts every Monday."

And we shook hands.

She waved my twenty dollars. "I got the best of you. I would have settled on one free donut."

I sniffed. "You only think you did. I'll pick your donuts because you didn't bother to mention that in your deal."

Her big grin exploded into a marvelous, raucous laugh, and I joined her.

Her son delivered my chairs to the shop that afternoon. "Mama said you got the last word on that donut deal. Good job. I've never known anybody to get the best of Mama." He chuckled. "Makes you a town celebrity. You better get ready for your donut business to explode."

After the young man left, Woody said, "You got the best of Aunt Gee, Miss Lady? That's..." He was interrupted by his coughing. "Sorry. Awesome. How do we celebrate?"

"Hmm. Let's pick out paint for the office. We need a nice color for a meeting room. Let's take the car."

When Colonel jumped onto the back seat, Woody slid in next to him. On our way to the hardware store, Woody asked, "What's a meeting-room color?"

I loved colors, but I wasn't much of a decorator. "Something cheerful. It should be light, so people can read, but it shouldn't be a color you'd see in places like offices, hospitals, or schools." *Or prisons.*

"No white or gray" Woody said.

"Right. And no tan."

"Pink. It's your color," he said.

"I don't know. I'd like it, but I'm not sure anyone else would."

Woody coughed and leaned on Colonel. "Not dark pink. Light pink."

What would people think?

"Miss Lady, are you thinking what other people would think?"

"Can I get back to you on that?" I was busted.

"I like it because it's you. Pink is nice." Woody sneezed then smiled.

"I'll bet we can find something we like."

We stood in front of the paint samples at the hardware store. Woody peered at the display and picked out six pink samples. "Has to be a real pink, not a pretend pink. These two have too much purple, this one is too bright, and this one has too much orange." He put the four samples back and handed me the last two. "You pick."

I frowned. "I was going to say that."

He chuckled.

I compared the two. "Either would be fine with me, but I think this paler one is the real pink we want."

Woody pumped his fist in the air. "Yes!"

I added brushes, cloth, and tape to our cart.

While the machine shook our gallon, the stocky young man at the counter said, "I like this paint."

"We got it for the meeting room, Andrew," Woody said. "We need a happy pink."

The clerk nodded. "Happy pink."

On our way back to the shop, Woody leaned on Colonel. Woody carried in the sack with our supplies, and I carried in the paint and tarps.

"Are you sure you're okay? I can contact the lady then take you to the doctor myself."

Woody coughed then said, "No, the man's here. She said she'd take me on Monday."

"I'll have the room painted by Monday. Take tomorrow off if you like and get well."

"Yes ma'am." He gave me a weak smile and shuffled to the door.

I scooted the buffet next to the table in the middle of the room and threw the tarps I'd bought over them then moved the chairs to the main shop. After I taped the baseboards, I stood at the door with my arms crossed. "I need an extension pole and a ladder. And a nap. Let's go home, Colonel."

The next morning, I sipped my coffee while Colonel ate his breakfast. "I'm excited about painting today, Colonel. I've never painted before. How hard can it be?"

We arrived at the shop earlier than usual, and I inspected the office. "Looks ready to paint." I hurried to the storeroom to grab my apron. "Let's make pink pastry."

Colonel closed his eyes.

After I pulled out the last batch of cranberry scones, my phone rang. *Monica.*

"I'm leaving at noon to visit my sister in Savannah and will return Sunday night."

"Thanks for letting me know. I'm painting the shop office. I expect it will take me all weekend."

"Sorry I won't be around. I like to paint."

"I think I do too. Safe travels."

The bell jingled, and the sheriff came into the shop. He strolled to the reading table. "The chairs are a nice addition. You get them from Gee?"

I poured coffee and grabbed donuts and a scone for his plate. After I set our cups and his plate on the counter, I said, "She found them for me. Perfect, aren't they?"

The sheriff sat at the counter and peered at my face. "Everything okay?"

I frowned. "Woody's sick. He's got a terrible cough. He's supposed to see the doctor on Monday."

He turned toward the back of the shop. "What are you doing in Otto's office?"

I glanced at the room. "I forgot to close the door. Amber asked for a meeting room for her book club and other small groups that don't have anywhere else to meet. Woody and I picked out the paint yesterday, and I'll paint it this weekend." I rose and closed the door.

Sheriff stared at his plate. "Let me guess." He closed his eyes and rubbed his forehead. "I am thinking. Just a wild guess, you and Woody picked out pink paint." He peeked at me and grinned.

I snickered. "Why do you say that?"

"Psychic. The pink sprinkles on the first donut and strawberries in the classic white glaze on the second donut had nothing to do with it. However, I did consider the pink drizzle on the scone as a potential clue."

He laughed, and I joined in.

After the last customer left, I cleaned the shop then Colonel and I went to the hardware store and bought a ladder and an extension pole for my paint roller. Andrew carried the ladder out to the car.

"Haywood is sick," he said.

"Yes. He's going to the doctor on Monday."

Andrew frowned. "Haywood is sick." Andrew shook his head and returned to the hardware store.

He's concerned too.

Colonel and I went to the house, and I had a quick lunch then changed to painting clothes. I had planned to leave Colonel at home, but he guarded the door.

"If you go, it's not my fault if you're pink when we come home."

He nudged the door, and we returned to the shop.

By dark, I had painted one wall. "I'm done for today. I hope I can finish this before Monday." I cleaned my brushes and roller then we left for home.

I woke at four. My arms, back, and legs ached as I stumbled to the kitchen to make coffee. I fed Colonel and Mia and sat at the kitchen table to drink my coffee, but when I rose to refill my cup, the stiffness in my back and legs slowed me down.

I let Colonel out for his break and stayed by the window while he checked for early squirrels. *I sure hope I loosen up enough to finish painting today.* After I let Colonel back inside, I refilled my cup and hobbled to the sofa. "Do you think I'll be able to get back up?"

Mia jumped on the sofa and stretched across my usual seat.

"You're right, Mia. I'll see if a shower helps."

I felt better after my shower. Colonel and I left for the shop at six. *Later than I expected.* By noon, I had the second wall and half of the third painted. I sat on a reading chair for a break and drank another glass of water.

By four I painted the last wall and all the trim, washed my brushes and the roller, and loaded my supplies, paint, and tarps into the car. I stored the ladder in the storeroom and left the door open for the paint to have more circulation for drying.

When Colonel and I were home, I unloaded my car and put everything away while Colonel napped.

I planned to review my spreadsheet and spend a little time on the computer that evening, but I was so exhausted that I couldn't even read. I went to bed at eight-thirty.

―――― *ele* ――――

I was still sore when I woke Monday morning. *I'll be okay in a week.* I moaned as I dressed.

After Colonel, Mia, and I arrived at the shop, I checked the window for Woody while I mixed the dough. "He should have been here by now."

I covered the dough with a tea towel to rise. "Come on, Colonel. Let's go find Woody."

We walked up and down the block in the dark. "You know what, Colonel? I don't even know where he lives."

My chest tightened, and I felt lightheaded. I reached for a nearby fence to steady myself. I took in a deep breath through my nose, held it, and exhaled through pursed lips. My breathing slowed, but my heart still pounded.

My mind raced. *What if he just took the day off? He's a kid, and he didn't feel well on Friday. Maybe the lady is taking him to the doctor today. If I call the sheriff or contact the school, Woody could get into trouble. Besides, what would I say? But what if he's hurt?*

I took another deep breath to slow down. *I'll wait until this afternoon. He'll be here. I know it.*

The air in the shop was sticky, oppressive, and weighted down with worry. The shadows covered the front window. Mia meowed. Colonel paced. I finished up the donuts, but when I turned to set them in the display case, I tripped over Colonel and hit my face on the corner of the counter. I wrapped ice in a dishcloth, held it to my cheek, and hoped the ice would minimize the swelling.

I noticed I'd poured strawberry syrup into the classic glaze. I tossed the improvised ice pack into the sink, and in my hurry and frustration to dump the pink donuts and make a new batch, I stuck my finger into the glaze. I licked the sweet strawberry icing off my finger.

"Mmm. Not bad at all."

I placed my newest creation into the display case and wrote on the overhead chalkboard menu *NEW Classic Strawberry Glaze*. Mia entwined herself between my legs. I swooped her up and carried her while I prepared to open the shop. I didn't need a second fall.

The sheriff came into the shop earlier than usual. I poured his coffee and put the cup in front of his favorite seat.

"What happened to you? You've got a black eye."

"Tripped and hit my face. Been a while since I had a black eye. Is it bad?" I touched my fingers to my cheek.

"Yes. You need to tell people you got the last beer."

He frowned and cleared his throat. "On a serious note, Haywood wasn't at the Dixons when the caseworker went to the house earlier this morning for a follow up. Mr. Dixon said he and his wife talked about

Haywood going to foster care, and Haywood must have run away."

"Foster care? Why would they do that?" My escalating panic turned into rage, and I was incensed. *Woody doesn't belong with strangers. His rightful place is with people who love him.* I felt the heat rush to my face. I clenched my fists and scowled at Grady.

"The caseworker said she wanted to talk to Harriett Dixon, but Ronald was vague about where she was. The caseworker asked to check the property for Haywood, and Dixon refused. She will talk to her supervisor about next steps."

"Are they even related? What right do they have to send him away? Why foster care? Where would he go?" My voice grew louder and higher in pitch. I wanted to run out the door, find Woody, and make sure he was safe.

"I don't know. This is a real mess. I'm not sure where the state would place him. No openings for a permanent foster home for kids his age. Might be a few temporary places around Atlanta. They're overcrowded too, but it's short term. Maybe a few days. Or a couple of months. Hard to say."

My head spun. *Woody was just a boy. He had done nothing to deserve all this.* I moved to sit on the closest stool and lost my balance. I would have fallen if the sheriff hadn't caught my elbow and steadied me. "Easy."

"What about his father? Where is he?" I pulled my arm away.

"Josh was a Federal Marshal, and a fine one too. Drug cartel ambushed and murdered him and two other marshals when Haywood was three."

"What?" I was a little hurt Woody hadn't told me, but to be fair, I never told him my husband was dead or how he died. "What does it take to be a foster parent?"

"Ms. Karen, I know you're upset, but this isn't anything you can take on."

"Yes, I can. What does it take?"

"The process takes about three months." The sheriff sighed. "Training, criminal check, house inspection. That's it."

"Okay, thanks. Let me know when you find him. Promise?"

"I will."

I scowled when Shirley rushed into the shop. *Not in the mood.*

She peered at the display case. "Strawberry glazed? That sounds good. I'm trying to cut back, so one donut and a scone for me today."

I poured her coffee and handed her the sack with her pastries.

Shirley cleared her throat. "Sometimes I might say the wrong things. I hope this isn't one of those times. I heard about Woody and the Dixons, and I was angry."

Before I could say anything, she grabbed her coffee and dashed out of the shop. I stared at the door then closed my mouth. *Didn't expect a nice Shirley.* A tear slipped down my cheek as I placed more donuts into the display case.

After I closed the shop for the day, Colonel and I strolled to the grocery store. I spotted a tin superhero lunch box on a top shelf. Tears blinded me. *Woody deserves a superhero lunch box. And somebody to pack his lunch for him.* My peripheral vision blurred, and I felt light-headed. I clutched the grocery cart to keep from dropping to my knees.

"Ma'am, are you okay? Can I help you?" I raised my head and saw a stock boy who stood next to the shelf with a concerned look on his young face.

I straightened my back and took a breath. "Can you reach that lunch box for me?" I pointed to the top shelf.

He handed me the lunch box. "This one?"

"Yes. Thank you for your help."

He nodded and turned away. He glanced back at me, and I waved.

That evening, Colonel and I strolled to the shop. I put a small brown paper sack with a note, *On your side. Miss Lady,* and a drink, two donuts, and a hard-boiled egg into the new lunch box at the back door of the shop.

The next morning, I rushed to the shop and unlocked the back door. The lunch box was where I left it. I opened it and stared at the sack. *Untouched.* I stumbled inside to my reading chair and sobbed.

I shuffled through my morning tasks.

"You okay, Ms. Karen?" Sheriff asked after I poured his coffee.

"Allergies are getting me down. I couldn't sleep." I turned back to the display case.

"I'm worried about Haywood too, Karen."

My tears welled up at the sound of concern in his voice.

Later, Shirley rushed in and grabbed her sack and coffee. "Gotta run. See you tomorrow."

I slumped against the counter in relief.

After my last customer left, I called to ask about an application for foster care.

"Ms. Donut Lady, the form is online. Shall I send you the link?"

"Yes, please." I gave her my email address. *Thank you for helping me set up email, Max.*

I refreshed the contents of Woody's sack that afternoon before I left the shop and trudged home.

When I climbed into bed, my soft sheets were scratchy. I punched and fluffed my pillow, but I couldn't adjust it to a position that didn't give me a kink in my neck. I clicked on the light, propped my pillow against the wall for support, and reached for a book that was on my bedside stand. My back ached, so I turned off the light.

I screamed and when I sat up in bed, the shadows in the hall scattered. Colonel rushed to my side, and I trembled and wrapped my arms around him. I didn't remember any details of the nightmare, but I knew I needed to escape. I swaddled myself in a quilt, and Colonel and I slept on the floor.

Pain in my left hip from the hard floor woke me, and Colonel and I hurried to leave the house.

"Shall we walk or drive?" I asked.

Colonel trotted to the car and sat outside the driver's door.

We arrived at the shop an hour earlier than usual, and I rushed to the back door. I gasped at the sight of a piece of a paper with a smooth rock on top of it. I unfolded the paper and read the single word, BOOK. When I checked the lunchbox, the sack was gone. I startled Colonel and Mia with a whoop. "He took the sack and left a note!'"

Colonel trotted out to the porch, and I rubbed his ears. "I have a note from Woody. He wants a book." Tears rolled down my face in relief, and Colonel leaned on me. "I miss him too, boy."

We went inside the shop. I waved the note and danced, Colonel barked, and Mia skittered to the storeroom. I hummed while I mixed my first batch of dough.

"Let's celebrate. The sheriff's favorite donut is pink-sprinkled, and mine is maple. We haven't made cinnamon donuts in a while, and everyone loves them. Shirley likes the blueberry scones. We'll make a treat for Shirley too."

I fried donuts and donut holes then while my scones baked, I sprinkled and dipped the donuts. After the donut holes cooled, I shook them in a brown paper sack along with the sugar, cinnamon, and a smidgeon of cayenne pepper that Mr. Otto called his magic dust for happy customers.

When the bell jingled and the sheriff sauntered in, I'd made coffee and filled the display case.

"What's up today?" the sheriff asked as I poured coffee.

"I have your pink-sprinkled donuts and special donut holes with magic dust."

"Sounds like what I need to tackle my day." He sat at his usual spot.

I refilled his cup then ran hot water into the sink. The sheriff sipped his coffee while I scrubbed pans. "Glad to hear you applied for the foster care program training. You may want to talk to the county attorney too. It's good to stay occupied. It'll help take your mind off Haywood."

I shook my head. "I think about Woody all the time. Where is he? What's being done to find him?"

"Gotta run."

"Stinker," I said to the door.

Shirley swooped into the shop. "You look awful. You have sunken eyes and black circles under your black circles. Are you sleeping? Eating?"

Sometimes I just didn't have the energy to deal with Shirley. *Like now.* "I'm fine."

"Are not. Come to my house for dinner tonight. Six o'clock. Don't say you're busy because you're not."

One thing about Shirley. She was consistent; she said whatever popped into her head with no filters.

"You're still bossy." I tried to smile. No success.

She straightened her back, puffed out her chest, and grinned. "I know. Aren't you proud of me? What do you like to eat? Oh, never mind. Doesn't matter. I can only cook a couple of things and all of them are frozen meals. You don't have any allergies or anything, do you? Do you like red or white wine? You can bring Colonel if you want to. I wouldn't want him to be lonely. Mia's okay by herself, right? Bring her if she wants to come." She grabbed her coffee and donut and left. *Maybe partially mellowed.*

"White," I said to the door. *One way to get the last word.*

After the last customer left and the shop was clean, I left Colonel and Mia at the shop and dashed to the bookstore.

"I heard Woody was missing," Cathy said as she joined me in the graphic novel aisle. "I feel awful. Are you okay? What can I do?"

"I'm trying to stay busy. I don't know what else to do. Can you help me find four or five books as a surprise for him?"

Cathy rushed to the register and returned with Woody's list. "Let's find some that aren't on his list."

After we picked out five books, Cathy added them to the bottom of Woody's list. "So we don't forget when he picks out more books," Cathy said with a smile.

I hurried back to the shop and made another sandwich and sliced more cheese. I added a donut, a banana, and a drink to the sack then closed it inside the lunchbox. I slipped the book under the tin box then Colonel and I went inside the shop.

I unzipped Mia's carrier. "You going or staying, Mia?"

Mia batted the carrier door closed and marched to the storeroom.

"Don't blame you. If you see Woody, ask him to stay on the porch."

After Colonel and I were home, I fed him then I went back over my Yakima data and compared it to Knoxville to find any similarities. At dusk, I stretched and turned off my computer. *Nothing.*

Colonel and I strolled to Shirley's place. The sky was pale orange with wisps of high, feathery clouds; the temperature had cooled down enough for jeans and my favorite pink sweater over my pink-checked shirt. Colonel wandered from yard to yard on our way and left a trail of yappy dogs inside the houses we passed. I brushed away a tear as I walked. *I'll always appreciate fresh air and the freedom to stroll with my dog anywhere and anytime.*

When we reached Shirley's apartment, she threw open the door before I knocked. She wore a black skirt and heels with her signature red jacket over a white blouse.

"You look very nice, Shirley."

Her hand fluttered to her hair, and her face turned a soft pink. "Thank you. I don't entertain much. I was nervous. My first dinner party. Thank you for coming. You too, Colonel."

Shirley grilled...more accurately, burned...a burger on her indoor grill for Colonel. Colonel didn't care.

"Colonel likes his burgers charred," I said.

"Charred. Thank you," Shirley said with a blush that started at her neck and flamed up to her face.

After we sat at the table, I shook out my napkin and smoothed it on my lap. "Your red woven placemats and turquoise cloth napkins are very festive with your terracotta plates, Shirley. Feels like a party."

"Thanks, I've tried to brighten up my life a little. I heated the frozen lasagna in my oven, and I didn't burn it. Did you know white wine is good with lasagna because of the ricotta cheese?" Shirley placed the lasagna on a hot pad in the middle of the table.

I blinked. *She's not joking.* "I didn't know that."

For dessert, Shirley dished up butter pecan ice cream in blue bowls.

"Shirley, I forgot how much I love ice cream." I sipped the rest of my glass of wine with dessert.

"Champagne and ice cream," Shirley said. "White wine counts as champagne."

I forgot how goofy Shirley can be and how much she made me laugh when we were kids.

The night air was cooler than I expected on our walk home. I stretched my stride, and Colonel trotted alongside me. By the time we reached the house, I was breathless and energized. "Good exercise, Colonel," I said as I unlocked the door. "But I need a warmer coat for our evening walks."

The next morning, Colonel and I hurried to the car. When we reached the shop, I unlocked the front door and rushed to the back door. The book was gone. I opened the lunchbox, and the sack was gone. I sang a nonsense happy day song and danced. Colonel barked and Mia hissed.

I laughed. "My singing's not that bad."

Mia hid in the storeroom, and Colonel flopped down near the front door.

I dropped my last batch of donut holes into the fryer as the bell jingled, and the sheriff strolled in. I poured his coffee, served him a pink-sprinkled donut, and rushed back to the fryer.

"This was supposed to be a sleepy little town, Ms. Karen." The sheriff rubbed his hand across his face, sipped his coffee, and took a bite of donut. "Mmm. Coffee and a warm donut. Fixes everything."

"That's why I bought the donut shop." I poured myself a cup and perched on the stool next to him.

"Too much going on. I appreciate that you don't badger me for information, although I have one piece of information that I can share with you. Did you know the Dixons left town? Turns out they didn't leave together. Harriett Dixon took the little girl to her daughter's house in South Carolina the week before Haywood disappeared. Her daughter's a minister. The girl's mother is Mrs. Dixon's niece, and the parents are out of the country. I think on a mission trip. Harriett Dixon heard I was looking for her and called me late yesterday."

My heart was racing. "What about Woody? What did she say about Woody?"

"She said her husband was going to take Woody to the social worker the day she left. We know he didn't."

"Why did she leave?" I narrowed my eyes. I glanced at the sheriff's empty cup and grabbed the coffee pot.

"She was a little vague at first. Thanks for the coffee. Can I have a scone? Then she told me she left because Dixon drank up all their money. I asked her if he got mean when he drank, and she said no. She said he was a lazy bastard, and when he was drinking, he was a lazy drunk bastard. Excuse the language. Her words." He shook his head. "I'm not sure I believe her."

"Suppose I could call her? Ask her about Woody?"

"I'll give her your number. I'll ask her to call you. I don't know if she will. She claimed she didn't know anything."

I wrapped his scone and dropped it into a sack. He opened his sack and breathed in the aroma of the warm pastry. "Strawberry. Yum." The sheriff finished his coffee and donut. "So what's new with you, Donut Lady? I've been talking my head off."

Woody, shadows, nightmares. Patterns of death.

"I went to Shirley's for dinner last night. When Colonel and I walked home, it was cooler than I expected. Are we in for a cold snap?"

"According to the weather, we've got cold weather headed our way." His radio crackled. "I better settle up. I'll take my scone for my mid-morning snack."

After the last customer left, I scrubbed pans. "I'm worried about Woody. I hope he's warm. How do I find him, Colonel?"

Colonel and I walked downtown. When I stepped into the boutique for a coat, the soft fragrances of lavender and peach greeted me. Shirley told me Whitney took over the boutique after her mother died last year. She'd updated the shop décor and clothing.

"I need a coat." I glanced around. *Fancy shop.*

Whitney laughed. "You're lucky. Mama kept records of the weather so she could shop for what her customers would need at the last minute. I've changed a lot of things around here, but Mama's drive to have what her customers need is in my blood." She pointed at the coat rack near the wall. "Let's find you something you like. What are you looking for?"

"Something warm with a hood and long enough to cover my behind. Functional, not fancy."

"Wish I had something in pink. Here's a dark rose. That's close."

I tried on the coat, and it was a little large and the sleeves covered my palms. The lining was a fleecy rose and gray plaid flannel. "Soft. I like this. Large enough for extra layers underneath Do you have gloves?"

"Try these. Driving gloves, but they're lined."

I put on the black gloves. "Love these. They'll be warm. This was easy."

"Anything else you need today?"

"That's it." *Woody.* "I'm sure Woody needs a winter coat. What do you have?"

"Over here." She strode to the other side of the store. "How about this olive-green coat? If it doesn't fit, just bring it back."

She folded the jackets and slid them into sacks.

While she finished up our transaction, I said, "I'm used to going into a store looking for a coat because it's cold and finding bathing suits."

Whitney laughed. "Mama said that's why she opened up the boutique."

We stopped at the house, and I packed a sandwich, apple, and a second drink in a lunch sack then Colonel and I walked to the shop. I left the coat, another book, and a sack on the back porch. Mia dashed out of the storeroom and flicked her tail.

"Mia, I wish I could hide to see Woody, but I don't want to scare him away. And what if it's somebody else? I think I don't want to know. Do you see Woody?"

I lurked around the shop until close to dusk then I dragged my feet in my reluctance to be away from the shop while Colonel explored along the way home.

The county attorney, John Padilla, called as I reached the house. "Ms. O'Brien, I have a copy of your court records. Would you be available for a chat tomorrow? Say two o'clock?"

I poked my fork at my baked chicken and rice then wrapped my plate and put my food in the refrigerator. I tried to read, but my mind was on Woody.

Before I went to bed, I let Colonel outside for his break. My throat seized at the coldness of the night air.

When I woke at three-thirty, I had tossed off my covers. I reached to the floor and pulled up my blanket.

Wonder if Woody has his jacket?

Chapter Seven

Colonel and I rushed through our morning routine and were on the road to the shop before four. When I unlocked the door, Colonel and I dashed to the back door. My heart sank when I saw the jacket. Colonel and I searched around the back and sides of the shop.

"Maybe Woody didn't notice the coat. Let's check the lunch box."

We returned to the back of the shop, and when I picked up the lunchbox, I burst into tears. *The book. Woody would have taken the book.*

I carried the lunchbox inside and tossed the perishable food then mixed my first batch of dough. "I don't feel very chipper, Colonel, and I can't think of one donut that sounds good. Maybe I'll just make plain donuts and scones. Maybe I'll just put a sign on the door saying we're closed for the day. What's the saddest donut? Something downright blue."

Colonel lumbered to the storeroom, and Mia dashed out.

"That's it. Blue. Blueberries. But the sheriff has to have sprinkles." I climbed up on my stepstool and found blue sprinkles.

When the sheriff came into the shop, he stared at the display case. "Blueberry donuts and scones, and you even have blue-sprinkled donuts and blue donut holes. How'd you do that?"

I poured two cups of coffee and placed his at his usual place. "I found blue sugar on the top shelf in the storeroom where Mr. Otto hid his offbeat ingredients. I think he didn't want his accountant to know how much he spent on random items."

He gulped down his coffee. "I get it. Blue. You're sad, right?"

I set his plate on the counter with one of each kind of pastry. "You're right. It was the only way I could think of to get through the day." I refilled his coffee.

"I'll start with the sprinkles; which one are you going to try?"

I stared at him, and he chuckled. "You're blue, not me. Pick one."

I put a scone on a plate and sat next to the sheriff. "Do you have any news about Woody?"

"Not really, but my gut says Woody is close. What do you think?"

"Makes sense to me, but I have no idea where."

The sheriff's radio crackled. "I'd rather stay here and be blue, but I gotta go."

When Devlin's son picked up their donuts, he said, "Me and my friends are searching for Woody. Just letting you know."

"Thanks." After he left, my eyes welled up from the kindness of Devlin's youngest son and his friends.

The bell jingled, and Giselle came into the shop. When she glanced at the display case, her mouth shifted from a grim downturn to a weak smile. "You feeling blue, Donut Lady? I'm right there with you." She perched on a stool at the counter. "Coffee and a scone, please."

After I poured two cups of coffee and served her a scone, I sat next to her.

She bit into her scone. "Mmm. This is good. You added a little lemon to it? Bright taste."

We sipped our coffee in companionable silence, and when I refilled her cup, she cleared her throat.

"I stopped by to tell you one of my son's sketchier acquaintances told him he saw Harriet Dixon leave town in the middle of the night. He was vague about when that was, but Isaiah got the sense it was over the weekend. She had a little white girl with her. No Woody. After Mrs. Dixon left, this guy looked in the shed. I think he planned to steal something, but that's not the point. He said it looked like somebody stayed in the shed. I think Woody's in town somewhere, but I don't know where. My boy Isaiah and I checked the parks and a few other places early this morning."

"Do you think he hid because he heard the Dixons talk about foster care?"

Giselle raised her eyebrows. "Is that what the Dixons planned? To turn him back over to the county? There are terrible stories about kids in foster care, but Woody was already in foster care at the Dixons. It's hard to say what got into his head."

I gazed at Giselle. "When he disappeared, I left him food and a drink near the shop's back door. I know he picked it up because he asked for a book when I checked Wednesday morning then the book was gone yesterday morning. I left him a warm coat yesterday, but it was still there this morning." Tears welled up.

"His clothes..." My voice cracked.

Giselle shook her head. "Threadbare. I worried about this cold snap too. We'll keep looking and praying."

I was at the county attorney's office a little before two. He waved to his small conference table. "Please have a seat. I've been reading over your records."

I was impressed he didn't feel the need to keep a big desk between the two of us. *Me being a murderer and all.* I frowned at the bitterness I didn't realize I carried. Maybe I need to give Shirley a little slack.

He sat next to me at the table and dropped a large file folder on the table. "What do you remember about your trial?"

"Not much. It was all a blur. I was pretty numb."

He nodded. "Will you be okay if I give you my impressions of the file?"

"Absolutely."

"The prosecutor had an easy case. A woman with a history of violence against her husband runs over him with her car in cold blood. At least, that's the prosecutor's case. Did you know that?"

I rubbed the back of my hand with my fingers. "I think I did, vaguely. It wasn't a surprise because my husband worked hard to create a trail of his abuse by my hand."

John looked puzzled. "I'd be very interested to hear how he did that if you don't mind."

"It was fairly simple. It started when Terry said..." My voice failed, and I took a breath.

I glanced at my intertwined fingers in my lap and cleared my throat. "He said some disgusting things. I wanted to get away from him, and he stepped in my way, so I pushed past him. He broke his arm when he fell. He laughed and called the police. He told them I knocked him down and broke his arm. I was arrested. He refused x-rays. Said he'd see his own doctor."

John shook his head and spoke almost to himself. "Handled as a he-said-she-said case and ignored the unsubstantiated broken bone. Too bad nobody picked up on that."

I nodded. "After that, Terry injured himself with surface injuries and complained of pain. He'd go to the doctor or emergency room and tell them I did it, but he'd say I didn't mean it. Or something like he was trying to cover for me. I lived in terror of what he'd do next."

He pointed at the file. "Your attorney was not very aggressive. He was either disengaged or lazy. I'm not sure which one. For sure incompetent. I was surprised he didn't even call you to testify in your own defense. Did you refuse? He didn't present much of anything, except witnesses who said you were a nice person, which you are. That's probably the only solid fact in this whole file."

"My lawyer said I shouldn't testify. I'd make things worse."

John tapped his fingers on the table and frowned. "Well, I'm not sure how much worse he thought it could be."

He walked to a file cabinet and pulled out a folder. He placed the folder on the table in front of me; it was my application to foster.

"The law is unambiguous. As a convicted felon, you can't be a foster parent. However, as a friend, I suggest you hire a good lawyer. I can give you some recommendations of lawyers I would use."

My heart sunk. *I should have known I couldn't pass a criminal check.* "Thank you. I'd appreciate it."

He wrote down names and numbers of three lawyers and gave me his card. "I'd be interested in who you talk to, and if you have any questions at all, feel free to call me."

We shook hands. On my way home, I realized I wasn't ready to call a lawyer yet. *Woody first.*

On my way into the house, I pulled the mail out of the mailbox then dropped it on the kitchen table.

I scrubbed a potato, slathered a chicken breast with barbeque sauce then popped them into the oven. After I fed Colonel, I turned on my laptop to do a little research.

While the computer ran through its startup process, I flipped through the day's mail and tossed each piece into the trash until I came to a letter addressed to *Teach.*

Inside the envelope was a smaller envelope with a typed letter inside it.

Teach

I hope you get this letter. A guard mailed it. I will be released next week and need to talk to you because I know who killed Shorty. Duchess said you live in Ohio. I will come see you. Enclosed is my sister's address. Write to me there.

Twitch

The address was a post office box in a small town near the prison. I snorted. *This isn't from Twitch. The killer's getting sloppy.*

The shadows billowed from the hallway and rattled the living room windows. I stared, and the shadows disappeared.

I rose from my desk and plodded to the kitchen then wrapped my leftovers in foil to warm in the oven. I went outside with Colonel while he wandered the yard. *I don't understand the shadows.*

After I ate, I searched hiking deaths around Yakima, Washington, and found tragic results, but the pattern was hiking in unsafe areas, not murder. I read until I was exhausted then dragged myself to bed.

I pulled up the covers then tossed them to the side. I flipped to my right side and punched my pillow. *Is Woody okay? Why does the killer want to know where I am?*

Colonel laid his head on my bed, and I relaxed.

I woke to a rank odor. I sat up. *Shorty.*

"Where are you?" I asked.

"Right here. You can't see me. My voices want you to know Twitch fell."

Colonel whined, and the odor dissipated.

It wasn't a dream. I paced then curled up on the sofa, and Colonel jumped up and flopped on my feet.

At four o'clock, I fed Colonel then dressed. I snapped a photo of the letter with my phone and grabbed my pink sweater for the chilly morning air. Colonel and I trudged through the dark, silent neighborhoods to the shop. *Too late for the crickets and katydids and too early for the birds.*

When we reached the donut shop, we hurried to the back door. The coat, book, and sack lunch were still there.

I crossed my arms for warmth and stared into the dark. "All I can think about is Woody. I need pastry inspiration. Let's check Mr. Otto's recipe book."

"Chocolate chip scone. That's a new one for us. Woody would like it."

When the bell jingled at six, I poured two cups of coffee as the sheriff strode in. "Smells like a chocolate factory in here."

He perched on his stool and sipped his coffee. "I need to cut back. One of each. I'll cut back tomorrow."

He devoured his pink-sprinkled donut in three bites and gulped down his coffee. As I refilled his cup I asked, "Need another pink-sprinkled?"

"Not really. Are you feeling okay? You're pale this morning."

What do I say? A ghost told me an inmate died, and I got a letter from the dead inmate who couldn't read or write? And Woody doesn't have a coat.

"Just worried."

He picked up his sack and headed toward the door. "We all are."

I cleared the sheriff's cup and plate and finished scrubbing baking pans when my phone rang. *Giselle.*

"Any news?" she asked.

"Nothing. The coat's still there."

"I was afraid of that. I'll let you know if I hear anything."

After the last customer left and I'd cleaned the shop, Colonel and I headed to the library.

The logical person to talk to would be the captain at the prison, but Duchess said Shorty's voices said it was important to know where a person came from. *I don't know where the captain came from.*

The library door whooshed open. *Love that sound.* Monica beamed, and I mirrored her expression. She summoned a volunteer with her silver pen and jingling bracelets, and we hurried upstairs.

When we reached the meeting room, I said, "I love your pink blouse and your red jeans, but aren't they a little staid compared to your usual personal style?"

Monica busted out laughing. "You caught me. The Board of Directors met this morning, and I presented a proposal for more books for reluctant readers and a room dedicated to them and our volunteer reading assistants. They agreed to my proposal. Thanks for the idea."

"That is heartwarming news."

"What do you have?" she asked.

"An unusual question. Where are you from?"

"I'm from right here. I was born in a farmhouse outside Asbury, and except for my college years, I've been in Asbury my entire life. Shorty's voices, right?"

"Yes. Duchess told me Shorty's voices said it was important to know where a person was from. I took that to mean from a trust standpoint. We never talked about the outside, but Duchess told me Shorty was from Tennessee, and she was from West Virginia. I told her I was from Georgia. I don't know where Twitch was from, but I know she couldn't read. She was able to parrot words, but her retention was poor. Those are the facts. Read the note." I pulled up the picture on my phone and showed Monica.

She exhaled a low whistle. "On the surface, this is an inmate reaching out to someone she most likely admires. But knowing that Twitch was illiterate, the note screams desperate killer, doesn't it? Is there anyone you can talk to at the prison?"

"The captain at the prison gave me his cell phone and said I might need a friend, but I don't know where he's from. Another person is the prison librarian, but I don't know where she's from either, and I don't like her."

"That's reason enough. What about the sheriff?"

I rose and wandered to the window. My eyes widened as a young mother folded her oversized stroller with one hand and opened the back hatch of her minivan with a push of a button. When she and her wiggly toddler reached the side door, it slid open and she secured her child in a car seat. "The technology changes in the past twelve years amaze me."

I returned to the table. "I don't know how to explain to the sheriff that the voices a dead woman heard are my advisors on who to trust. I need to keep digging so I have concrete evidence."

I drummed my fingers on the table then folded my hands on my lap. "Shorty was from Tennessee, and our first group of deaths were in Knoxville. What if Shorty was from Knoxville and knew the killer? My stumbling block is I don't know Shorty's name outside of the walls."

Monica tapped her pen. "I'll see if I can find anything."

"I thought of something. I wonder if the captain has a resume online? And the librarian too. I'll see if I can find anything."

"More steps forward. I'll check to see if she applied for any library positions." Monica headed to the door, and I followed her down the stairs.

Three women and the volunteer at the desk whispered and giggled in a huddle. When Monica tapped her pen on the railing, her bracelets jangled. The three visitors scattered, and the volunteer hurried to pick up the books on the counter.

"Never gets old," Monica whispered, and I snickered.

That evening, my anxiety increased as the shadows billowed and dominated the hallway. I read later than usual to avoid them. I woke on the sofa with a crick in my neck and my book on the floor. I picked up my book, trudged down the hallway, and flopped into bed.

What was that sound? I rolled over. I was back in prison, and it was dark. The person in the cell next to me screamed. "Hide, hide. They're coming."

A nest of baby birds was on my cell floor. My door sprung open, and a dozen inmates pushed and shoved into my one-person cell. I snatched up the baby birds and stuffed them into my shirt. Inmates screamed. "Hide, hide. They're coming."

They fought with knives and fists to get on the top bunk. "Don't let your feet touch the floor. They're coming."

The mob pushed and shoved me, and I fought to get to the top bunk too. More bloody and bruised screamers poured into the cell. Someone chopped off my arm, and a dog licked my face.

What? My groggy state of mind tried to explain why a dog was in my cell. *And where is my arm? I need it.* The dog licked my face again. I opened my eyes. Colonel's paws were on my bed, and he licked my face a third time. I touched my arm. It was wrapped in the sheet, and I was lying on it. I reached for the baby birds. My blanket was bunched at my chest.

"Good boy," I sobbed. "Thank you."

Sweat soaked my pajamas, my drenched hair stuck to my neck, my bed was a wreck, and my pillows were on the floor. Colonel and I spent the rest of the night on the sofa.

When I woke Sunday morning, it was six o'clock, and Colonel was asleep on the floor next to the sofa. After I fed Colonel and drank my coffee, I showered, dressed, and threw my bedding into the washer.

"Let's check on Mia." I picked up my car keys, and Colonel bumped the front door with his nose.

When I opened the shop door, Mia strolled out of the storeroom and stalked Colonel. I rushed to the back door and the coat and book were still there. I opened the lunchbox, and the sack was as I left it. I removed the sack and tossed the sandwich and cheese into the trash.

"It's only been two nights. Two cold nights." I rubbed my forehead, and my stomach churned.

I called Giselle, and her phone went to voicemail. "It's Karen. I'm at the shop, and the coat is still out back."

Early Monday morning I threw on my clothes and hurried to leave. "Let's take the car, Colonel. It's faster." I rushed to the shop's back door and checked. My phone rang before I closed the door. *Giselle.*

"Anything?" she asked.

"Coat's still here. It's been three cold nights. I'll talk to the sheriff when he comes by this morning."

"I'll help however I can."

A tear slipped down my cheek. "I know. Thanks."

When I saw the sheriff's car pull up, I plated two donuts, poured a cup of coffee, and waited for him to sit. The sheriff strode in and took his usual seat. "Lightning fast service this morning, Ms. Karen. You waiting for me?"

"I need to tell you something. I've left a snack on my shop back porch every evening since Woody disappeared. Sometimes it was gone. Sometimes it was still there in the mornings. It hasn't been touched in three days. Just wanted you to know."

While I started another fresh pot of coffee, I thought about hiding in the storeroom, then my thoughts drifted to what if I found Woody there, stocking supplies as if he'd never left? I swallowed hard and turned to face the sheriff.

"I suspected you'd do what you could for him. If he's close, I wonder if the Dixon relatives know where he is. I'll talk with his caseworker to see what she knows. May send a deputy out to check."

"Thanks, I'd appreciate it."

After Sheriff Grady left, I said, "Not as bad as I thought it would be. He didn't yell at me." Colonel wagged his tail. Mia head-bumped my leg. *Nice to have in-house support.*

The bell at the door jingled, and Shirley hurried into the shop. She wore a black skirt and her red signature jacket over a white blouse. *Maybe she'll grab her coffee and donut and go.* I poured her coffee and mixed in her milk and sugar.

"On your way to a meeting, Shirley?"

"How'd you know? What made the sheriff rush out of here? Did they find Haywood? Did he rob a house?"

Shirley brushed past me to pick up her coffee on the counter.

I slammed my hand down on the counter, and Shirley stopped her reach for her cup midair and stepped back.

I burned inside. *Slow down.* I took a breath before I spoke.

"The sheriff's a busy man. Sometimes he's in a hurry. Woody's a good boy, and I won't have you speaking poorly of him in my shop. If you can't restrain yourself, don't come in. I know it's hard for you, but you need to stop your negative thoughts. You're a good person, and other people are nice just like you."

She turned to face me and put her hands on her hips. "You don't know that, Karen. You've never been cheated on and tossed aside."

"You know I have, but that doesn't matter. You didn't deserve rotten treatment, but that was years ago. We were in high school, for goodness sake. Let it go or be angry at the world; I don't care. Just don't take your anger out on others in my shop. Be nice or leave."

Shirley gasped, and her eyes widened, but she didn't say anything else.

I handed Shirley her coffee and dropped her donut into a sack. She slammed the shop door as she left, and the bell clanged.

I collapsed on a stool. *So much for my resolve to give Shirley some slack.* Everyone had a piece of anger or sadness hidden inside. I wanted the shop to be a place of refuge, a place where it's okay to be kind.

"Be Kind Donut Shop. What do you think, Mia?"

Mia flicked her tail and purred while she licked her paw.

"I'll take that as agreement."

The bell jingled, and Amber approached the counter. She wore a black suit, and she had pulled her hair back into a bun. *Court day.*

"I don't mean to intrude, but I just heard about Haywood. I'm so sorry. I know you must be worried sick."

I swallowed hard and nodded. "Thank you. Would you like to see the meeting room? Woody picked the color, and I painted it."

When I opened the door to the office, her face lit up. "This is awesome. Absolutely the best meeting room I've ever seen. Let me know when you're ready to rent it. I know the book club will love the pink room. Maybe it would be fun to hold a grand opening when you're ready."

I nodded. "When Woody gets back, we can throw a grand opening party."

At the end of the workday, I set Mia's carrier near the door. "Want to go along?"

Mia rocketed to the storeroom, dashed out, circled the counter, then marched to her carrier.

After I parked at home, my phone rang as I lifted Mia's carrier out of the car.

Monica. When I answered, she said, "Join me for lunch at the library. Bring a sandwich."

"Be there in less than an hour."

After Colonel and Mia were settled in the house, I headed to downtown at a quick pace to stretch my legs.

While I waited in line at Gus's to order a turkey sandwich, the good-natured banter among the cooks and the counter workers lifted my spirits, and I smiled at their silliness then blinked at the realization. *Counter worker. Desk duty.*

After I paid for my lunch, I hurried to the library. *Shorty had regular desk duty.*

Monica wore black jeans, a transparent white blouse with flowing sleeves, and a bright yellow T-shirt under her blouse. She flicked her wrist, tapped her silver pen on a book, and her bracelets jangled.

A man with thinning gray hair rushed to the desk with two women behind him. His face was flushed. "Ready for desk duty."

"Well done. I have a meeting. You're in charge."

He saluted and turned to empty the book drop box while the two women scowled and stormed away. "Cheater," one woman mumbled.

"Let's have lunch in my workroom." Monica led the way to the older part of the library.

I expected a cramped, musty space with no windows and little light, books stacked on every horizontal surface, and a desk with papers piled high and overflowing to the floor.

When she opened the door, a sweet lilac fragrance welcomed me, and my eyes widened at the polished wooden desk with a computer and a lavender candle in a jar, a small round table between two matching Queen Anne chairs with a soft green background and tiny pink roses, and a dorm-sized refrigerator.

A white and sky-blue oval braided rug added depth to the dark wooden floor. Half of an emerald green rowboat with its bow pointed to the ceiling and its wooden seats turned into shelves was upended behind the desk and displayed books and colorful plastic dinosaurs. A helix-shaped chandelier with dangling crystals and silver balls illuminated every corner of the room. I blinked as Monica lit the candle on her desk with a flick of her pen.

Monica chuckled. "I work best in whimsy and colors if I can't be outside."

My shoulders relaxed. "I didn't even realize how tense I was until I walked in. This is an amazing room."

She opened her refrigerator and pulled out a sandwich and a bottle of sweet tea. She pointed to the chairs. "Make yourself comfortable. I thought you might like a little company."

When I sank into the chair, its wings wrapped me in a hug, and my worries slid away.

"Chair grab you?" Monica pulled two coasters out of a drawer in the small table, placed her tea on a coaster, and unwrapped her sandwich. "Are we going to divert from murders to finding Woody?"

I wrapped my drink cup with a napkin to catch condensation and set it on the coaster. "I'd loved to if I had any ideas." I unwrapped my sandwich. "I trust the sheriff and his deputies, and they are searching for him."

"More of them than us too." Monica bit into her sandwich. "Mmm. Have you ever had a peanut butter and pickle sandwich?"

"I don't think so. Sweet and salty?" I bit into my turkey and cranberry sandwich. "My sandwich is smoky and tart."

Monica sipped her tea. "What's on your mind other than the opportunity of a most enjoyable lunch?"

"The prison librarian, Charlotte, didn't have volunteers; instead she scheduled prison trustees for desk duty in the library."

"Makes sense." Monica polished off one half of her sandwich.

"What information would a trustee like Shorty have access to when she had desk duty? I know the trustees could search other libraries for books. I assume that would be by the internet but maybe not."

"It's hard to say, but it is likely a savvy trustee could access the internet in addition to any information on the computer that wasn't password protected."

"I don't know what Shorty's computer skills were. Mine are weak, but I wasn't interested in any of the offered online computer courses. Shorty might have been. Internet access explains how she had all the locations and dates. I'd wondered about that because she'd been in prison longer than I was." I munched on my sandwich.

"Search history is saved by the browser, but I'm assuming it would be meaningless to anyone except the killer. Searching the internet would not be out of line in a computer class. I wonder if the library computer had access to staff records? My computer in my office does, but I always log out because my volunteers can use my computer if the one at the desk is busy."

"When Charlotte let me use her computer, she was on top of me the entire time, but that was after Shorty died. Maybe she was paranoid. Too bad we don't have contact with anybody on the inside who could do some checking for us." I finished off my sandwich.

Monica rose. "Care for a homemade brownie for dessert?" She grabbed two brownies out of her refrigerator then paused. "What did you say?"

"Somebody on the inside?"

"I'm despondent." Monica handed me a brownie wrapped in plastic. "I've officially lost my membership card in the Donut Lady Investigative Society."

I giggled. "What are you talking about?"

"My favorite cousin is a corrections officer. I can ask her anything."

I bit into my brownie. "Mmm. You're officially reinstated."

"I can ask about the online computer access in the classrooms and who has access to personnel records. What else?"

"How to find out an inmate's name outside of prison."

Monica waved her silver pen. "Shorty and Duchess, duly added. Speaking of names, have you searched for the names of staff members online? You may find previous addresses."

I stared at her. "Now I've officially lost my card. I'll do that this evening."

"You're still in. The Donut Lovers Investigative Society has risen from the ashes of the dishonored members." Monica snickered when I choked on my tea.

Monica frowned. "Is the sheriff investigating Harriet Dixon? I'd heard she allegedly went to visit her sister, the minister. I know for a fact her sister is in prison."

I raised my eyebrows. "I'll pass that on to the sheriff."

As we headed to the door, Monica said, "Thank you for trusting me."

I nodded and bit my lip to keep from sniveling and embarrassing myself.

That evening, I settled on the sofa with a blanket, a cup of hot tea, and a new graphic novel. I intended to lose myself in the book, but thoughts of Woody and all the horrible things that might have happened swirled in my head, and I shuddered. Colonel eased next to me, and I rubbed his ears, relaxed, and read.

I jumped with a start when Colonel sprang off the sofa, scrambled to the front door, and barked as the doorbell rang. I peeked out. The sheriff stood on the porch. I opened the door and gasped at the dark look on his face.

"Can I come in?" he asked. "I need to talk to you before anyone else does."

I sat on the edge of the sofa. He sat in the chair and faced me.

He cleared his throat. "I sent two deputies to look for Woody. When they got to the house, it was empty. We hoped we'd find Woody there." He narrowed his eyes. "I have more. You okay?"

I'd never be okay until Woody was found, but I nodded.

"It looked like somebody had been staying in the Dixons' shed for an extended time. My deputies found a torn, dirty blanket and two lunch sacks. The lunch sacks were folded in a corner."

A chill hit the back of my neck, and I bit my lip. "What about a book? Did they find any books?"

Grady shook his head. "No books. Ms. Karen, do you need somebody to stay with you? Or could you go somewhere so you won't be alone tonight?"

Tears slid down my cheeks, and my voice cracked. "I've got Colonel. I'll be fine. Thank you."

After the sheriff left, Colonel jumped up on the sofa with me. I rubbed his ears and stared at the wall in disbelief. *Why can't anyone find Woody?*

When Colonel prodded my arm with his wet nose, I woke. I rose and stretched then headed to bed where I snuggled under my covers. I listened to the clicks of Colonel's paws on the hallway floor as he traveled to the kitchen then returned to my bedroom. After Colonel flopped on the rug next to my bed, he fell asleep, and I relaxed at the sound of his rhythmic breathing.

I hurried down a long, dark hallway. Colonel was at my side, and I carried Mia. We would find Woody. A pale glow at our feet lit the path ahead.

The hallway became a narrow trail on the side of a mountain. I put Mia in my backpack and held onto Colonel's harness. A faint light glided in front of my feet then the mountain shook and rumbled.

The narrow path turned into lava, and I struggled to pick up Colonel. I lifted him high to keep his feet from dragging on the ground. The lava burned the soles of my feet then the flames rose to the level of my ankles. Colonel squirmed, but I wouldn't let go. I wouldn't let him be burned.

We had to find Woody. When I looked down, my legs were in flames. Soft sobs intensified to screams, and I gagged at the stink of burned flesh. The ground shook and burning timbers crashed around me.

I woke to screams and grabbed the side of the shaking bed. The screams were mine. Colonel nudged me and bumped the bed. I patted my legs in case any fire lingered then rolled to the edge of the bed to hug Colonel. The shadows at my bedroom door darkened and billowed into the room, and I gasped in fear for Woody.

"What do you know? Where is Woody?" I collapsed on my bed in a torrent of tears. After my sobs and breathing slowed, I raised my head and glanced at the clock. *Four o'clock.* I dressed and thought about my dream. *This one was different.*

I grabbed a sheet of paper and a black marker and printed in bold letters, *Closed for The Day.*

"Let's put this note on the shop door, Colonel. I have an idea. Want to go, Mia?"

Mia lifted her nose and flicked her tail as she strutted to the pantry.

Before we left the house, I tossed a few things into my tote bag: a couple of bottles of water, a blanket, a banana, antiseptic, and bug bite medicine. As I walked out, I grabbed a couple of sofa pillows.

Colonel loved to walk, but he adored the car more. I opened the passenger's door and patted the seat. "Let's go."

I stood back. Colonel zoomed past me and did a high airborne leap into the car. He sat with pride in the driver's seat. I nudged him when I eased into the car. "Move over, bud. Let's go find Woody."

After we reached the shop, Colonel waited for me in the car while I taped my sign to the door.

We headed out of town. It wasn't far, only three miles. I turned at the former Carruthers house driveway and slowed. We crept past the scorched ground and the remnants of a brick fireplace chimney. The lone structure was a monument in the charred ruins. I scanned the farm for a shed. I squinted at the shed near the homestead ruins and a second structure farther away.

I parked, and Colonel and I climbed out of the car. The brisk north wind made the chilly morning bone-cold and took my breath away. The light of early dawn appeared on the horizon.

"Find Woody, boy," I said. Colonel stayed next to me. *Am I wrong?*

"Of all times for you to decide to guard me, Colonel. Okay, we'll walk together."

At least I don't have to carry my seventy-pound dog.

I pulled on the padlock at the first shed. *Locked.*

Colonel raced to the second shed and whined. I stared at him through my tears and stumbled to the shed. When I threw the door open, black shadows that filled the interior raked my legs and face with icy tendrils as they slid past me. I gaped at Woody's small body. He was sprawled face down like someone had tossed him into the shed or he'd crawled there.

I stepped inside and knelt next to him. *At least he's sheltered from the wind.* When I touched his back, intermittent gasps and gurgles came from his chest. I shifted my feet and slipped on a paperback.

"Woody?" I rubbed and patted his back, and Colonel prodded him with his nose.

I eased him over to his back and squatted to cradle his head against my arm. When I lifted his torso to drag him to the car, I was shocked at how light he was. If I were taller and younger, I could have carried him. I pulled him to the back seat and threw the blanket over him.

I grabbed my phone. "Tess. Tell the sheriff I found Woody. At the old Carruthers place. And send an ambulance. He's unconscious and having trouble breathing."

I elevated his head and shoulders with the sofa pillows, and the quality of his breathing improved. His filthy clothes smelled foul, and the bug bites and scratches on his hands and face bled and oozed. Colonel and I climbed into the car. I cuddled Woody and the pillows, and Colonel positioned himself to lean against Woody.

"Smart move, Colonel." I sniffled back tears and wiped my drippy nose on my sleeve. "He needs a fast warm-up, and you're the best."

The ambulance team scooped up Woody and sped away. By the time I turned the car around, they were out of sight. I rolled down the passenger side window, and Colonel howled his German Shepherd siren.

The sheriff met Colonel and me at the hospital. The empty ambulance sat with its rear doors open at the emergency entrance, and its interior lights attracted moths that swarmed and flitted in the patient compartment.

I called Giselle. "I found Woody. We're at the hospital; he's sick."

"I'll be right there."

I paced while the sheriff spoke to the clerk at the Information Desk.

"They know we're here. Might be awhile before we know anything," he said.

Giselle rushed into the hospital and took my hand. "How is he? What did the doctor say?"

"So far, nothing."

Chapter Eight

Giselle and I sat together near the Information Desk. We flipped through the waiting room magazines, shifted in our seats, and paced. Colonel stayed at my side, and the sheriff glowered and stood with his arms crossed near the desk.

After an hour, the sheriff left and returned with coffee from the nearby convenience store. "The hospital has coffee, but it's bitter. This isn't bad, and it's hot." He handed Giselle and me each a large cup, and we drank in silence.

A little later, the sheriff's phone rang, and he stepped outside. I stared while he stood with his back to me. He shook his head after he put his phone away and plodded into the hospital.

"My deputy thinks Haywood hiked from the shed at the Dixons to the farmstead three or four days ago. That's a long way for a sick boy."

Giselle finished her coffee and stopped at the Information Desk after she threw her cup away. She returned to her seat and shook her head. "Still nothing."

After another hour, I stood to stretch my legs, and Giselle joined me.

"I'd suggest we go for a walk..." the sheriff began.

A doctor in blue scrubs and a white jacket came through double doors, and the sheriff rose to stand next to Giselle and me.

The doctor lifted his glasses, rubbed his eyes, and approached us. "Haywood has a high fever and pneumonia and is still unconscious. He's a very sick boy. His age is an advantage, but he has signs of chronic poor nutrition. We'll know more about recovery when we see how he responds to treatment, but for now, we're worried."

I was ready to bust through the double doors. "Can I see Woody?" I asked. "Can I stay with him?"

The doctor glanced at Giselle. "Only one person can go. That okay with you, Ms. Gee?"

"I'll wait. Donut Lady is his best friend." The sheriff put his hand on her shoulder, and Giselle patted his hand.

The doctor nodded. "You can go in for a short minute, Ms. Karen, and you'll have to wear a mask and gown. We don't want him to get any sicker. We'll see how he does the next couple of days."

When I entered the small room, the regular sounds of automatic beeps greeted me. I searched the adult-sized hospital bed with its crisp sheets for the helpless boy among all the machines and tubes. I picked up his limp hand and covered it with mine. My heart melted. *He is so thin.*

After five minutes, which felt like five seconds, Woody's nurse touched my shoulder. "It's time to leave."

I rose. "Be strong, Woody. I need my reading buddy."

Giselle, the sheriff, and Colonel waited for me in the hall.

"How is he?" Giselle's face reflected my worried heart.

"Need a ride home?" Sheriff asked.

I shook my head. "I've got my car. He's so sick. He didn't wake up or say anything."

"Doc said I can see him later. I'll wait," she said.

When Colonel and I returned home, we sat on the sofa. "Woody's sick, but he'll get well."

I rubbed Colonel's ears, and my tears flowed. Colonel licked the tears that fell on my arm, and I hugged him. I called Monica then paced.

While Colonel inspected the backyard and I watched the birds at the feeder, Giselle called. "I saw Woody. He's so sick."

I sniffed back my tears. "He will get better. I know it."

"You're right. That child has his daddy's energy and his mama's gumption."

I have to do something. I spent the rest of the day cleaning and scrubbing my house.

The next morning, I woke to meowing. Colonel dashed out of my bedroom, and I threw off my covers and followed him to the kitchen. Mia was curled on top of the refrigerator. The shadows swirled on the kitchen floor and licked at the refrigerator. Colonel charged, and they dissipated. After Colonel had his morning break and I fed him and Mia, I dressed.

When I was ready to leave for the shop, Mia raced to her carrier near the door.

I opened the shop and unzipped the carrier. "I feel like strawberry drizzle today," Colonel trotted to his spot near the counter, and Mia pranced to the storeroom.

After I drizzled the last batch of donuts, the bell jingled, and the sheriff sauntered in. I plated his two donuts, poured our coffee, and sat at the counter with him. Mia slinked out of the storeroom and dashed behind the counter.

"Have a donut. They're good." He licked the dab of glaze off his thumb. "The sweetness has magic that will lighten your soul. Try it."

"I only eat..."

"I know. Have one for Woody. You'll feel better." He handed me his maple donut.

I took a bite. "The first donut I ever ate was when Woody and I ate maple donuts together."

His radio crackled. "Gotta go."

"One second." I grabbed a donut and a scone and dropped them into a sack. "For the road."

The sheriff saluted me with the sack and rushed out.

A few minutes later, I glanced at the front window. Shirley stood motionless on the sidewalk as she peered in the window. She wore black sweatpants and a red sweatshirt over a white T-shirt.

I squinted. *No makeup?*

She took in a big breath then dashed inside with her lips pursed. I poured her coffee and handed her a white sack with two donuts and a scone. She set money on the counter and hurried out.

"Do you suppose she's trying to be careful about what she says?"

Mia raced to the storeroom.

"Was I that cranky, Colonel?"

Colonel rose and joined Mia in the storeroom.

Max from the computer store sauntered into the shop. "I'm here under false pretenses. I need some advice, but I'm really here for donuts and coffee." He chuckled.

"I'll get your coffee and donuts. Have a seat." I smiled and waved at the counter. After I poured his coffee, I plated two donuts and a scone and poured a cup for me.

Max sipped on his coffee and ate his first donut. He wiped his mouth and picked up his scone. "Two years ago, I thought I might like to sell my store and move on. I listed it with a friend. There was a little flurry of interest but nothing serious. I'd forgotten about it. My friend called me this morning and said he had a potential buyer who planned to be in the area next week. He asked for a recommendation where his new client could stay. I'd heard you had stayed a night or two somewhere around here before you moved into your house. I was thinking about the newer place that has a new owner. What do you think?"

"Not the newer place. The Asbury Motel is older, but it has more amenities and the atmosphere you'd want a newcomer to town to enjoy. It might look a little rough on the exterior, but that's its rustic charm."

"Rustic. Got it." Max polished off his donuts, and I gave him a large coffee to go.

After the last customer left and I had put away the baking pans, I placed the cat carrier near the door. "You going too, Mia?"

She flopped down on the floor and glared at me.

"I'll take that as a no." I locked the shop, and Colonel went home with me.

"I'll eat lunch when I get back from the hospital. I need to check on Woody."

When I strolled past the nurse's station, a nurse called after me. "Ms. Donut Lady, I need to talk to you." She caught up with me. "Come with me to the visitors' room. We'll be more comfortable there. We can sit and chat."

I pursed my lips. *I don't like the sound of this.*

After we sat on the two soft chairs that were positioned for the medical staff to deliver bad news to a family member, the nurse put her hand on the arm of my chair. "Haywood had a rough night. The doctor moved him to the pediatric intensive care."

"What happened?"

"His breathing rate increased, and his breaths were shallow. He wasn't moving enough air. He's getting extra assistance with breathing now because he has a tube to deliver oxygen to his lungs."

"When can I see him?"

"Not sure. He needs a little healing time. I am so sorry."

"I can't see him today?" My voice had a catch in it.

"No. We need to keep him quiet until he's stronger. I'm sorry."

After she left, I slumped in despair. *Nothing I can do.*

My chest tightened with grief, and I dragged my feet on my way to the elevator and pressed the down button. When the bell dinged and the doors opened, I hesitated. A young man behind me cleared his throat. "You going down, ma'am?"

I don't want to leave Woody.

He caught the door before it closed and held it open for me. "Ma'am?"

I stepped inside. When the elevator bumped to a stop and the door opened at the main floor, he waited for me to exit. *Need to get home to Colonel.* I left the hospital and hurried home. Colonel greeted me with a wag.

"Sorry I was gone so long, boy. Shall we go to the park?"

Colonel danced and brought me his leash. We passed several neighbors who were mowing, trimming bushes, refilling bird feeders, or relaxing on their porch. Colonel yipped, and I waved as we strolled by. Four neighbors on our way to the park stormed inside their houses and slammed doors. *Can't get me down, biddies.*

Colonel found a stick and paraded around the park with it until a squirrel dared to set foot on a fence. Colonel tore after the squirrel. When the squirrel reached the end of the fence, it glanced back at Colonel, swished its tail then leaped to a tree. After it scampered higher, Colonel remained motionless as he stared up at the branches. The squirrel jumped to another tree, but Colonel continued his surveillance of the first one.

After ten minutes, I asked, "Ready to go home, Colonel?"

When he didn't respond, I clapped my hands to break his squirrel fixation and headed to the road. Colonel bounded after me. I set a faster pace than usual, and Colonel trotted alongside me. *Am I fixated on something that's not there?*

After we were home, I called the hospital to ask about Woody.

"He's holding his own, Ms. Donut Lady, but he's still too sick for visitors." his nurse said.

"Don't you think he'd do better if I were there so he'll know he's not alone?"

"He's never alone; he needs a few more days to become more stable."

"I understand."

No, I don't.

That evening, I searched for Captain Littlefield on the internet and discovered his wife was active on social media. I read about birthday parties, weddings, and baby showers complete with countless pictures of babies, families, dogs, cats, and food. Lots of food.

"I need a snack. You too, Colonel?"

I gave Colonel a treat then munched on crackers and sharp cheddar cheese and searched for more of Mrs. Littlefield.

She had an online photo album with thirty years of vacation pictures labeled *Travel Pictures*. She documented her three children as they progressed from preschool to college with hundreds of photos with the children and state welcome signs: Pennsylvania, New York, Oklahoma, Kansas, Colorado, Utah, North Dakota; my blurry eyes lost track.

"Too tired to care, shadows. Good night." I stumbled to bed, and Colonel followed me.

My alarm woke me, and I stretched. *No nightmares for a change.* I hummed while I made coffee and fed Colonel.

Before I left for the shop, I checked the forecast. "Eighty percent chance of thundershowers, Colonel. Let's take the car."

I pulled the last batch of scones out of the oven and waited for them to cool. As I drizzled the confection sugar and orange icing, the bell jingled, and the sheriff strolled into the shop. I poured his coffee and placed it on the counter while he examined the contents in the display case.

"How about my usual?"

"You mean your pink-sprinkled donut and another donut followed by whatever else I throw in your sack?"

He chuckled. "That's it. The usual."

He sipped his coffee. "How's Woody doing?"

"They say he's not well enough for me to see him yet. Maybe in the next day or so." I refilled his cup and filled one for me.

"Doc said he was one sick little boy." The sheriff finished his pink-sprinkled donut and broke his chocolate donut in half.

"I am anxious to see him." I rose to put donuts in his sack. "Don't suppose you'd raid the hospital to create a diversion so I could sneak in. I'll throw in an extra pink-sprinkled donut to make it worth your while." I wiggled my eyebrows.

The sheriff spewed his coffee. "Dang it, Donut Lady." He wiped his chin and the counter with a napkin.

He chuckled. "I will admit, but not in front of witnesses, that's the best offer I've had all day."

I refilled his coffee and sat on the stool next to him. "Did you hear Harriet Dixon's sister isn't a minister? She's in prison."

The sheriff frowned. "No, I hadn't heard that. I'll follow up." He drained his cup. "I hear a lot, but sometimes my position gets in the way, and I'm not as well-connected with the community as I'd like to think."

His radio crackled, and I poured coffee into a to-go cup then handed him his sack and coffee as he rushed out the door.

The bell jingled after I put his dishes in the dishwasher, and Shirley scurried in. She wore her work clothes, a black skirt and her red jacket with a white blouse. "I have a showing this morning in thirty minutes, and rain is headed this way. Who wants to look at a house this early in the morning in the rain? Not that I mind. I'd show a house with a flashlight at midnight if that's what a buyer wanted to do. I might have to borrow Mia for protection. She's a fierce little attack cat, isn't she?"

Mia stalked Shirley, and Shirley wiggled her fingers at Mia. "I've got my eye on you, cat."

Shirley stared at the floor. "You've taken lots of classes, haven't you, Karen? Is it hard? I signed up for a class. Do you think anybody will laugh at me? I'm not smart like you are. Things are hard for me to learn, and I don't like it when people laugh at me." She dropped her money on the counter and headed to the door.

"Wait a sec, Shirley. Here's your coffee and your sack."

She stopped and sighed. "See how rattled I am? My brain can't function this early in the morning." The bell jingled as she left.

I shook my head. "She's worried about that class, isn't she, Mia?"

The showers started at nine and continued through the rest of the morning. More customers braved the wet weather than I expected.

A little before noon, Devlin's son came in. "Mama wants to know if she could change her order to add an extra dozen donut holes? The little guys love the donut holes, and some of them ladies say they don't eat donuts and sneak a handful of donut holes."

I smiled as I boxed up Devlin's order. "I've heard that too. Makes me chuckle when somebody says they don't eat donuts then they order a half-dozen donut holes and eat them before they've left the shop."

He chuckled. "I'll tell Mama. She'll get a kick out of it."

After he left, I ran the dishwasher and swept the floor. *Woody swept the floor like a champ.*

I placed the cat carrier by the front door. "Who's going home with me?"

Mia marched to her carrier and disappeared inside.

"Let's go, Colonel."

When we stepped outside, it was sprinkling. "I thought the rain was gone."

By the time we reached the house, the sprinkles had turned into a downpour. I reached for my umbrella, climbed out of the car, opened the back door, and Colonel dashed to the porch. I opened the umbrella, but by the time I had lifted out the carrier, held the umbrella over the carrier, and closed the car doors, the torrential rain drenched me. I splashed my way through the puddles to the porch and unlocked the door. After I opened it, Colonel rushed inside.

"I don't suppose you could bring me a towel?"

Colonel shook and flopped on the rug near the sofa. I slipped off my shoes and left them at the door. After I released Mia, I dripped to the bathroom for a towel. I dried and changed to dry clothes then turned on the burner under the kettle for hot tea and called the hospital.

The operator routed my call to Woody's nurse. "He opened his eyes this morning. Check with us later."

I'd rather be on my way to the hospital.

After I made my tea, I turned on my laptop. "I need to stop staring up at the branches and shift to the squirrel. The branches are the falls the past twenty-five years. The squirrel murdered Shorty and Twitch and framed Duchess."

Colonel flopped on the floor next to me, and Mia scooted to the pantry.

I paced, and Colonel raised his head to watch me. "Is Duchess being framed because she knows something or because she was convenient?"

I opened a yogurt, swirled up a spoonful, and closed my eyes. *Mmm. Sweet peach and tart yogurt.*

After I scraped the last bit from the small carton, I plopped in my chair in front of the computer. I spent an hour in my search for Charlotte then started a pot of coffee. While it perked, I stared at the screen. I'd finally found Charlotte's current address. *This isn't any help. This is the address of the prison.*

I carried my coffee to the back door, and Colonel dashed out to guard his yard. While he patrolled, I pondered my options. *Maybe I need to talk to the sheriff.*

Colonel broke into my thoughts with a yip that was followed by a knock at the front door. I hurried back inside, and when I opened the front door, I almost dropped my cup. *Sheriff?*

"Sorry to startle you, Ms. Karen. I'm not here about Woody, just to let you know."

"Come in, Sheriff. Care for a cup of coffee? It's fresh."

He scrubbed his damp shoes on the mat and shook his ball cap.

"Rain's lightened up a bit. Coffee sounds good." He strode to the kitchen table and sat while I poured his coffee.

Does the sheriff have ESP?

I placed his coffee in front of him and joined him at the kitchen table.

He blew on his coffee. "Got a call this morning from a Captain Littlefield at the women's prison in Ohio."

I nodded. "I know Captain Littlefield."

"What do you think of him?"

"I met with him for approval for training tutors to teach reading. He approved the program." I narrowed my eyes, and the sheriff met my gaze. "He's a prison official."

The sheriff furrowed his brow and nodded. "I understand. Captain Littlefield asked if I knew you. I said I'd heard of you."

"Thank you. I'm not at the point of trusting him."

"The call seemed. Unusual." The sheriff drained his coffee and covered the cup with his hand when I pushed back my chair.

"He said he had an unofficial, confidential message for you but didn't know how to get in touch with you. I said I'd help. He promised Duchess he'd tell you that her handkerchief was overdue and so are your books. He asked Duchess what that meant, and she said *Teach will understand.* Do you know a Duchess? Does this make sense to you?"

"Yes. It does."

"Well, good." The sheriff held up his cup for a refill. "Now tell me what this is all about."

"You asked." I refilled both our cups. "Shorty heard voices and her voices told her things." I raised my eyebrows. "And they were always right."

I told the sheriff about Shorty, Twitch, Duchess, McMillan, Charlotte, and Captain Littlefield. I left out the shadows and the nightmares.

"I think Duchess believes Charlotte stole her handkerchief to implicate Duchess in Shorty's murder." I sipped my coffee. "If that's true, Charlotte murdered

Shorty and Twitch. Did the captain say anything about Twitch?"

The sheriff's eyes narrowed. "He said Twitch died in a fall, but I didn't realize the connection when we talked. How did you know she was murdered?"

"Shorty's voices. I think Charlotte's a serial killer." I reached for my phone. "Here's the note Shorty left on my cart in the library the day she was murdered."

I showed the sheriff the photo and told him about my Knoxville research results.

He rose and strode to the back door. "This is really far-fetched. Send that to me?"

"On its way." While I sent the photo to him, he drummed his fingers on the door jamb.

He exhaled and faced me. "You have no evidence."

"Correct."

"What about the rest of the addresses and dates?"

"We found twelve deaths in the Pittsburgh area from unwitnessed falls between the dates listed by Shorty. We haven't finished the searches, but that's just more circumstantial evidence."

"And of course, you can't leave this alone, can you?" Sheriff narrowed his eyes. "Wait. Duchess said your books were overdue. Does she think you're next on Charlotte's radar?"

"That's my interpretation."

"So what do we do?" The sheriff rubbed his hand through his hair. "This is all circumstantial."

"Let me check something." I hurried to my computer.

While I searched, Sheriff peered over my shoulder. "You're researching yourself?"

My eyes widened. "I never realized how much of my life is on the internet." I scooted back in my seat. "Might not be much longer before she shows up. Charlotte knows my name. She knows where I am."

"I can call Captain Littlefield to let him know I passed on the message. I can be subtle and ask if their librarian is a state employee or a contractor and whether she's still there. What else?"

I frowned. "Shorty said something about a friend. Let me check something." I searched for Idella Violetta Gold birth records in Knox County, Tennessee. "Look at this. Idella Violetta Gold would be forty-seven. Ivy Gold. Shorty called her Poison Ivy."

"I can see if Ivy Gold has a criminal record. Can you send that to me?"

I forwarded the record to the sheriff. "Done."

Sheriff finished his coffee. "Thought I was dropping by to deliver a message. Didn't know I would leave here with a heartful of worry."

"Sorry, but thanks for your help."

Sheriff paused at the door and growled. "You'll let me know if you see or hear of Charlotte, right?"

"Of course, I will."

"I mean in advance. Not after she's attacked you."

I rolled my eyes, and he shook his head and left.

I called Monica and left a message on her voice mail. "It's Karen. I'm checking in to see if you have anything."

When the rain stopped, Colonel and I stepped outside to the backyard, and birds chirped and sang in the trees. Cardinals flitted from the trees to the grass around the birdfeeder as a lone female pecked and tossed seeds to the ground. Her mate perched on the nearby fence to guard her. After the cardinals flew off, sparrows gathered around and under the birdfeeder and snacked on the smaller seeds.

"The birds are celebrating the end of the rain." I breathed in the cleansing aroma of wet grass and fresh air. "I needed this, Colonel. Let's go for a walk around the block."

Colonel trotted a zig-zag pattern to clear the path of any squirrels. Each squirrel dashed up a tree and scolded Colonel with its chatters. He sat motionless with his head up and dared the squirrel to touch the ground again. When I caught up with him, he dashed to the next squirrel on the ground, and they raced to the next tree. I sped up my pace for the cardio benefits, and by the time I reached the house, the exercise and fresh air had elevated my heart rate and my mood. Colonel and I added another half block to cool down. When we returned home, I filled Colonel's water bowl and poured a glass of sweet tea for me. I leaned against the sink while Colonel drank his fill.

"We should do this every day, shouldn't we?"

Colonel wagged his tail and flopped down on the cool kitchen floor.

My phone rang. *The hospital.* In the few seconds it took for me to answer, my emotions flipped back and forth between excitement because I would see Woody and despair because something bad had happened.

When I answered, the nurse said, "Ms. Karen, we're moving Woody this evening. The doctor removed his breathing tube, and he's been stable. We'll observe him the rest of the day to be sure he stays stable then move him out of the pediatric ICU."

"When can I come visit?" *Now?*

"We hope to have him moved by six, but if it takes a little longer, you'll need to wait. Or if you prefer, we'll call you after he's settled."

"I'll be there at six. I don't mind waiting."

After we hung up, I dropped onto the sofa and cried with the excitement and joy of seeing Woody soon. *Nothing else matters. Only Woody.*

My phone rang. *Monica.*

"Sorry," she said. "I had meetings all day. Why don't we meet tomorrow at Ida's for lunch? One okay with you? Or would two be better?"

"Sounds great. One o'clock is fine. The hospital just called me, and I can see Woody this evening."

"That's excellent news. I know you must be relieved. See you tomorrow."

I fed Colonel and Mia at five and checked in with the Information Desk at the hospital at five-thirty. I held my book open on my lap but kept my gaze fixed on the Information Desk except for an occasional glance at the first sentence in my book. At six, I approached the Information Desk.

"Sorry, Ms. O'Brien," the clerk spoke in a soft voice. "No one has called yet."

"Thank you. I think I'll move closer." I pointed to a seat near the Information Desk.

"I'll come get you as soon as I hear anything."

Ten minutes after six, the sheriff sat next to me. "Nothing yet?"

"No."

"I talked to Captain Littlefield. He's a good guy. Charlotte walked out without giving notice last week. The contracting company is scrambling to fill her position. Wayne, Captain Littlefield, was happy to see her go but furious she didn't give notice because of the impact on the inmates. He doesn't have the manpower to staff the library. The warden ordered an audit of the library and of the contracting company's hiring practices at Wayne's request. Wayne asked the contracting company for a copy of her resume. He'll get me the given names for Shorty and Duchess tomorrow morning. Tess is checking Ivy."

A nurse stopped at the Information Desk and spoke to the clerk. I inhaled when the clerk rose, but she shook her head then motioned to a young couple who sat in seats on the other side of her desk.

"I called the FBI," the sheriff said. "They'll send an agent out to talk to us. You have any ideas on how I can explain Shorty and her voices?"

I smiled. "I suggest not mentioning them. For all we know, Shorty shared what she knew by claiming the voices told her."

"True. That helps, thank you. They'll want to talk to you before they leave."

"I'm not surprised. Is it possible you could be there when they do?"

"It depends. I'll ask. Did you walk?"

"No. I'm parked in the south visitors' lot."

"Let's move your car closer."

"But what if"

"Go get your car, and I'll stake out a parking place for you. I'll tell the Information Clerk to come get me. Deal?"

"Deal. Be right back."

Sheriff rose to head to the Information Desk, and I hurried to bring my car around to the front. When I returned with my car, the sheriff guarded an empty parking space in front of the hospital. I parked and jumped out.

"Anything?"

"Not yet. I'm not staying but let me know if you need me."

Chapter Nine

Ten minutes after the sheriff left, Woody's nurse led me to the elevator to see Woody. On the way up, she said, "Remember, he's been very ill. He's still not very responsive. He hasn't opened his eyes yet, but he is doing great. He's breathing on his own. That's huge. We think he can hear us, so talk to him. You going to be okay?"

"I'll be fine."

"You have five minutes. I know it's short, but we're hoping he knows you're here. We'll push for more time every day. You ready?"

"I'm ready."

She stopped at a closed door. "You're important for his healing." She tapped on the door and pushed it open. This time, I was prepared for the machines and tubes and oversized hospital bed. I wasn't prepared for how frail Woody was.

I scooted the chair close to Woody and patted his hand. "I brought your favorite book. I can only be here for five minutes so I'll read the first one or two pages this time."

The nurse tapped on the door while I was reading the second page. "Five minutes, Ms. Donut Lady."

I closed the book and patted Woody's hand. "I'll save our place and read more tomorrow, Woody. Have a nice night."

When we stepped outside the room, the nurse said, "Did you see him responding to you? He relaxed when you started reading. His mouth twitched when you read *Geoff never got into trouble on purpose.* All big steps for him this early."

After I reached my car, I glanced to my right as shadows in a nearby grove of trees parted. I squinted at a figure exposed by the shadows' movement. I blinked, and the figure was gone. *I'm tired.*

―――*ele*―――

The next morning Colonel, Mia, and I went to the shop. As I mixed the dough, I glanced at the front window where a figure seemed to lurk where the shadows gathered. *Is someone there?* I frowned and the shadows floated to the road. *No one there.* I shrugged and left the dough to rest while I started the first pot of coffee. *Must have been remembrances of Woody.*

The bell jingled. "How's Woody?" the sheriff asked before he closed the door.

I poured two cups of coffee and plated donuts for the sheriff. "He is so frail. I was allowed only five minutes. I read to him, and the nurse said he responded to my voice." I set his coffee and plate on the counter. "Thanks for coming to the hospital."

"I have news for you. I have Shorty's name, and something I can't tell you about Duchess. Take my maple donut. This is a doozy."

I reached for the donut and took a bite. "Okay." I mumbled with my hand over my mouthful of pastry.

He drained his coffee cup and grinned. "More, please?"

"You are dragging this out on purpose, aren't you?" I grumbled as I refilled his cup.

"Duchess was undercover..."

"No!"

"Yes. She was undercover, and you have to forget you know this. They needed to pull her out when Shorty was murdered, and the fastest way was to charge her. Shorty's and Twitch's murders are under investigation. And before you ask, I wasn't told what Duchess was investigating."

"I'm still processing that Duchess was undercover. She was good."

The sheriff shook his head. "I can only imagine the bravery it would take to be undercover in a prison. Must have been important."

"Wonder if..."

The sheriff scowled. "Wonder nothing. Forget it."

"You're right. Done."

"Here's Shorty's name." He slid a piece of paper across the counter. *Idella Violetta Gold.*

I stared at the paper then belly-laughed so hard that I slipped off my stool. The sheriff laughed too but caught me before I slammed to the floor.

"What a hoot that Shorty was. Best way ever to let me know what her name was." I wiped my eyes. "Shorty was Poison Ivy."

I snorted-laughed and fanned my face with a napkin. "Is that confidential?"

"No. But this is unless you run across an old newspaper article. It was quite the sensation twenty years ago."

"What are you talking about?"

"Ivy Gold was convicted of murder twenty years ago."

"Seriously? And who did Ivy Gold poison?" I hurried to the coffee pot to refill my cup and returned to my seat.

"Her husband and her husband's brother. Her father-in-law died at the same time from a heart attack. He died with an empty medicine bottle clutched in his hand. Heart medicine."

"I'll bet she had a great motive."

"I'll bet you're right."

"It's her business. Not anything for me to broadcast, but Monica has been helping me with research. Monica will appreciate it. Now I wonder if Shorty's voices were real." I cackled, and the sheriff snickered with me, or maybe at me.

He glanced at the clock. "I need to get back to my paperwork. Do me a favor and be careful. You need to be around for Woody."

I glared at him as he left. *Now I have to be careful on top of worrying about Woody.*

Colonel and I left the shop at noon. After he had his break in the backyard, Colonel came inside for his afternoon nap. I reviewed the Knoxville and Pittsburgh data one more time. *This is curious.*

I printed my spreadsheet and added it to my folder then strolled to Ida's Diner with my folder in my backpack. I was ten minutes early, but Monica waved at me from a booth toward the back. I slid into the booth.

"How's Woody?" she asked.

"I saw him for five minutes last night and read to him. He'll be well soon, I'm sure of it."

"Know what you'd like?" our waitress asked.

"Special for me and sweet tea," Monica said.

"Same," I said.

After our waitress left, I whispered, "What is the special?"

"Who cares?" Monica snickered.

Our waitress brought our tea, and I gulped down half my glass. "I was thirsty. I've got a couple of interesting tidbits. I know Shorty's name."

"How did you do that?" Monica asked. "I haven't gotten anywhere."

"Ready? Put your tea down first. Her given name was Idella Violetta Gold."

"Poison Ivy?" Monica said in a voice loud enough to be a bellow. The diner quieted and the customers stared, and Monica tossed her head. "I have a cure for that."

I sneaked a peek and snickered as customers nodded. "Good recovery there, Monica. Not that I'm surprised."

"You caught me off guard. I'm sorry I didn't know Shorty." She lifted her tea in a toast. "Rest in peace, Shorty."

I nodded and lifted my glass then we clinked a toast to Poison Ivy.

"I have an interesting observation." I set my folder on the table. I set the spreadsheet in front of Monica and sat back in my seat.

She frowned at the sheet. "Women. They are all women. Why did we not see this earlier? Have you sorted the rest of the data?"

"No, I haven't. I didn't see it until I was ready to leave home then I was anxious to show you."

"After we eat, let's go to my office and check the other four locations."

"I'm not sure what this proves, but the sheriff called the FBI. He might like to have this. One other thing: Charlotte left the prison library with no notice."

Our waitress refilled our sweet tea glasses.

"She doesn't appear anywhere in the records of hired or available librarians, which is highly irregular. Everybody's in that database."

The waitress set our plates in front of us. My mouth watered at the sight of chicken and dumplings with a fresh-baked roll and butter and the side dishes of butter beans and collard greens.

Monica waved her fork. "Let's eat."

We dug in, and when we were finished, we pushed back our plates. Our waitress hurried to our table with two slices of pecan pie and two cartons for takeout. She chuckled as she set down the pie and collected our plates. "Don't see many women clean a plate here. Y'all are awesome."

"Is that true?" I asked after she left. "I've never known women who left food on a plate."

"I'm with you. I've always eaten everything on my plate. The curse of having five brothers."

I chuckled. "Eat it now or somebody else will."

On our way to the library, I saw the shadows drift behind the hardware store as we turned the corner. After we sat in front of Monica's computer in her office, she asked, "Are you being followed? I thought I saw movement near the hardware store."

I rubbed the back of my neck. "I've seen shadows over the past day or so, but I put it down to nerves. The sheriff told me to be careful."

"I'll give you a ride home. You might want to keep Colonel close to you. He wouldn't let anyone harm you."

"That's true. I'm ready to go whenever you can get away."

"Let's go now."

When Monica pulled into my driveway, she said, "You going to send the spreadsheet to the sheriff?"

"I'll pull it together and email it before I go see Woody."

"Good. Our next task is to stop Charlotte."

I opened the car door. "Any ideas on how we do that?"

"Because I always have books on the brain, what do you think about searching for Poison Ivy's yearbook? Want to race?" Monica winked.

"Glorious idea. You're on."

At five-thirty, Colonel and I went to the hospital. I parked close to the entrance and near a light pole. When we reached the entrance, Colonel assumed a sentry position next to the door.

When I came to the nurses' station, Woody's nurse waved me on and joined me as I reached his door.

"Ten minutes. Unless I get a little busy." She winked.

When I opened the door, I breathed in the fresh aroma of bath soap and lotion. Woody's scratches and bites had small scabs. I breathed in relief at the signs of healing.

"I'm back, Woody. Ready to read?" I scooted the chair closer to his bed and patted his arm. "You're looking better. Let's see what Geoff is up to."

After fifteen minutes, I realized the nurse stood in the doorway.

"Time." She smiled. "He relaxes when you are here. You bring healing book magic with you."

"Can I come in the afternoon and evening tomorrow?" I rose and returned the book to my backpack.

She snorted. "Pushing it, Donut Lady. Not quite yet, but soon."

When I stepped outside the hospital door, Colonel rose and pranced to the car. As we headed toward home, I said, "Woody's getting better."

That evening, I searched for high school yearbooks for two or three years around the time I guessed Shorty would have graduated. After an hour, I leaned back in my seat. "Ivy Gold, you were a pretty girl." I didn't recognize any of the other girls in her class. When I searched the next year, I found Charlotte. *Charlene Bowerton.* I searched for Charlene Bowerton on the internet with no results.

She might have married young. I rubbed the back of my neck. *I need a break.* I turned off my computer then dropped onto the sofa and opened my book. Colonel shifted from sleeping on the floor near my computer to the floor next to the sofa.

After I'd read for what seemed a short while, I glanced at the clock. *Midnight.* I flipped pages. *One chapter left after this one.* I read the last page and lumbered to bed.

The next morning, the sheriff came into the shop earlier than usual.

"Did you shift your routine, Sheriff?" I poured our coffee and set his plate of donuts on the counter.

He slid onto his stool. "Not my idea of a good time, but I've got a load of paperwork to catch up on at the office before I get distracted. Did you know it's a scientific fact that waving blades of grass are more interesting than paperwork?" He chuckled, and I joined him.

"Did you get my email?" I asked.

"I glanced through the spreadsheet. All the victims appear to be women, is that right?"

I refilled our cups. "Does anybody know Charlotte's real name?"

The sheriff gazed at me. "I'm having trouble with the anomaly of a lone female serial killer murdering random female victims, most likely strangers, using physical force. The pattern fits a male serial killer."

My eyes widened. "Pattern of death?"

"You might call it that."

"If the killer isn't Charlotte then who else could it be?"

The sheriff scowled. "Not for you to worry about."

I shrugged and started another pot of coffee. "Okay."

When I returned to my seat, the sheriff said, "I heard what you said. You're not going to worry, are you? You plan to pursue it."

I met his gaze. "Did you know you are a very suspicious man?"

He shook his head and rose to leave. "I don't know why I bother. My paperwork gives me plenty of aggravation with no backtalk. Be careful." He slammed the door on his way out.

"Have you noticed he gets irritated when he doesn't want to talk about something, Colonel?"

Amber came into the shop at ten. She wore her yoga shirt and pants, and her skin glistened with sweat. She flopped onto a stool at the counter, and I poured her coffee. "Scone and a maple donut, please. Yoga was a real workout this morning. You'd think I'd know better than to skip a month." She grabbed a napkin and wiped her face and neck. Mia skittered out of the storeroom and curled up at Amber's feet.

She bit into her maple donut and sipped her coffee. "Yum. Did you hear about Harriet Dixon? The authorities arrested her in Indiana for kidnapping. Turns out the little girl wasn't her granddaughter."

My eyes widened, and I dropped onto the seat next to her. "Really?"

"Shocking, right? A woman in yoga was talking about it. It's all rumor and conjecture, but allegedly..."

She stopped and gazed at me. "Is this too upsetting for you?"

"Not at all. Woody is safe and healing. Do you suppose that's why he hid in his grandparents' shed?"

"Might be. I'm thrilled to hear Woody's recovering. Great news." Amber finished her donut and bit into her scone.

"Yes it is. Indiana, you said?" I refilled her coffee.

"Indiana, yes. A hotel worker heard a little girl crying, and when she tapped on the door, there was no answer. She reported it to the desk clerk who called the police. When the police and the hotel staff entered the room, the girl was alone. She was dirty and stinky, which infuriated the hotel staff, according to my yoga informant. The police found Harriet buying beer at a nearby convenience store and arrested her. Most likely for child endangerment, but that's my lawyer-interpretation; gossip said kidnapping. This might be embellishment, but the girl was hungry, which is why she was crying."

"Wow. Do we know anything else? Was the little girl identified?"

"No. Maybe our local news will have something this evening. May I have another maple donut for the road?"

I placed a maple donut in a sack, and Amber settled her bill then left.

While I cleared the dishes, Peyton came into the shop and sat at the counter.

I waved the coffee pot. "Coffee?"

"No ma'am. I need to try all the donuts and a scone."

I put ice in a glass and filled it with water then put donuts, donut holes, and a scone on a platter.

She picked up a pink-sprinkled donut and held it up for inspection before she bit into it. "Yum. I love this." She took a larger second bite. "I really love pink sprinkles."

After she ate the donut, she picked up a cinnamon donut hole and ate it. "Wow. Crunchy and soft. I'm not sure I ever had a donut hole before. When I was younger, I thought a donut hole was a joke that grownups made up to fool kids."

"Are you doing a taste experiment?" I asked.

She giggled. "Kind of. I was supposed to order three dozen donuts for Mr. Dustin's birthday on Monday as a surprise from the whole team, but when I opened the door, donut munchies overcame me."

I chuckled. "That has got to be the best description I've ever heard of a donut craving. You are too funny."

Peyton grinned. "Thanks. I guess I'll order three dozen mixed donuts and two dozen donut holes and one scone for me. I'm supposed to pick them up early on Monday. Is seven too early?"

"Not at all. I'll have them ready for you." I rinsed the coffee pot while Peyton enjoyed her pastries.

As she munched on her scone, she said, "When I drove up, I saw a car parked at the vacant lot on the corner. I stared because it was a rental car that didn't come from us. I'm car-obsessed. Anyway, the driver looked angry that I stared or something, and she peeled out. No reason to abuse a car like that. I don't like her."

I bit my lip to keep from smirking. "What did she look like?"

Peyton frowned. "I'm better at car descriptions than people descriptions. The car was a Toyota four-door, this year's model, mileage less than two hundred miles, dark metallic blue that almost has a black shimmer, black wall tires, built-in backup camera, satellite radio, and a three-inch scratch on the back bumper. Oh. The woman was old. Like over thirty or even forty. She slumped in the seat, but she was tall."

I blinked. *Old? Over thirty?* "Wonder what she was doing?"

"I'd say casing the joint because I like to read crime novels, but there's nothing close except the donut shop. Maybe she pulled in to make a phone call."

"Probably so."

Peyton glanced at the counter. "Where's my ticket?"

"No charge," I said. "You were here on official taste-test business."

Peyton laughed. "Love it. Thank you, Donut Lady. See you on Monday."

After Peyton left and I'd cleared her dishes, I peered at the vacant lot down the street but could only see the building next to it. Not the best place for surveillance unless she had binoculars.

I was cleaning the counter when the bell jingled. Devlin's son sauntered in with a smile. "I hear Woody's doing great."

I boxed up the donuts and donut holes.

"We have a new guest. Mama said she wished you were there, so she'd remember there are nice, relaxed people in the world. This woman is a nervous and irritable diva. That's what Mama said. The diva is thinking about buying Max's business. She must have money because she drives this expensive-looking shiny black car."

The hair on the back of my neck rose, and my skin was prickly. "Toyota?"

"Yep." His face paled. "Oh no. You know her? Is she a friend? I'm sorry. Mama says I need to watch my mouth."

"No, I don't know her. I thought I saw a newish car downtown. Probably near the computer store."

"Mama said if that diva buys the computer store, I'm driving to Albany for all our computer supplies."

"What does she look like?"

"Tall and muscular like she works out. Old. Mama said her brown hair is dyed. She's jumpy and particular about everything. She asked Mama if she knew Teach. Mama said she knows a lot of teachers then the diva asked if Mama knew anyone named Karen. Mama said no and the diva ate two donuts."

"Why did Devlin say that?"

He laughed. "Mama told me later she was tired of the diva, and it's not lying when someone gets on your last nerve."

I chuckled. "Hard to argue with mama-logic, isn't it?"

He grinned and carried the boxes to the door then paused. "See you Monday unless Mama makes me stay with the diva. She almost came to pick up the donuts herself today."

I need to talk to Devlin about her latest guest.

After Colonel, Mia, and I were home, I poured a glass of sweet tea. Mia stalked shadows, and Colonel and I went out back. While Colonel roamed, I admired the next-door neighbor's camellias and the manicured lawn and bushes then glanced at my backyard. *Rustic.* I snort-laughed, and Colonel trotted to see if I'd found food or a squirrel.

"Sorry, boy. Nothing interesting."

On our way back into the house, my phone rang. *Monica.*

"Have you had lunch? I had a very interesting morning and need to talk to you but not in a public place. If I bring sandwiches, may I invite myself to your house? And bring someone with me? You trust me, right? Are you home? Do you keep donuts at your house?"

"No donuts here, but I have brownies and an interesting finding to share. Of course, I trust you, and you know how mysterious it sounds that you would ask. No, make that suspicious."

"Because it is." She cackled and hung up.

I pulled six brownies out of the freezer and spread a clean Thanksgiving tablecloth onto the dining table.

Mia marched out of the pantry with a look of disdain as she flicked her tail and licked her paw.

"It's the only tablecloth I have, Mia. If I'd had more warning, I could have borrowed Shirley's red placemats, except I think we're not speaking."

I sat on the sofa with a new book. Colonel jumped up and leaned against me then Mia jumped onto the sofa and lay across the pages.

Guess I'll pay attention to my animals instead. I scratched Colonel's ear and stroked Mia's back.

My phone rang. *Monica?*

"We're here. I trust you too."

This does not sound good.

The shadows that had been dancing in the hall disappeared. When the car doors slammed, Colonel lumbered to the door.

I opened the door, and Monica whispered, "Trust," as she breezed past me with two white sacks from Gus's.

Charlotte stood motionless in the doorway, and her face was pale.

I stared at her then glared at Monica who shrugged. "You would have said no. Am I right?"

"You're right." My voice was as tight as my mouth.

Colonel sniffed Charlotte's hand then assumed the heel position on my right. Mia strolled to Charlotte, turned her back to her and flicked her tail then sat on my left. Mia faced Charlotte as I stared at Colonel and Mia.

"I understand you two are acquainted. No introductions required." Monica opened kitchen cabinets. "Here they are." She pulled out three plates and set them on the table.

I cleared my throat and stepped away from the doorway. "Come in. This is Colonel, and this is Mia." I pointed to the animals. Mia dashed to the pantry, and Colonel stayed by my side.

Charlotte stepped inside. "I've been looking for you, Teach."

"Let's eat first," Monica said. "You have any sweet tea? I forgot about drinks."

"Glasses are there." I pointed to the cabinet next to the refrigerator while I pulled out the pitcher of tea. "Have a seat, Charlotte. Where are you from?"

"I'm from Pittsburgh." She sat, and I nodded. *No you aren't.*

"I got you a smoked turkey and cranberry sandwich, Teach. You going to sit with us?" Monica joined Charlotte at the table then parceled out the sandwiches and sacks of chips. "Gus refused to make me a peanut and pickle sandwich, but he made a plain peanut butter sandwich and gave me a container of pickles. If it gets back to him I told anybody, I'm banned from the sandwich shop." Monica snickered and added pickles to her sandwich. Charlotte stared at her plate, and I stared at Charlotte.

When Charlotte picked up her sandwich, I picked up mine. We ate in silence. After she ate her sandwich, Monica refilled our tea glasses. "You said you have brownies?"

I placed six brownies in the middle of the table, and Monica grabbed the largest one and bit into it.

"Yum. Charlotte came to the library this morning. She wanted to talk to you and someone at the grocery store told her we were friends."

"I've been looking for you. Shorty and I were friends…"

My eyes widened, and I raised my eyebrows.

Charlotte shrugged. "I know. I don't make friends easily, and I've got my rough edges, but we just hit it off. Shorty was from Knoxville, and Twitch was from a small town near Albany, New York. Twitch and I didn't get along. She rubbed me the wrong way and vice versa, but she was Shorty's friend so we tolerated each other. Shorty and I talked about everything. She mentioned some of her friends from high school had fallen and died while hiking alone. She said two of them hated the outdoors. It was strange, because the same thing happened around Pittsburgh, but not at the same time. Shorty talked to Twitch. Twitch is really superstitious. She was afraid if she talked about the deaths, death would hear her and come for her. But she told Shorty. She idolized Shorty." Charlotte shifted in her chair.

"Let's move to the living room. The furniture's more comfortable," I said.

Monica sat on the sofa and glanced at the side table. "I need a coaster." Mia jumped up on her lap.

I pulled three paper towels and folded each one into quarters. "Here you go."

Charlotte chose the chair, and I placed her folded paper towel on the table next to the chair.

"Y'all knew about three locations of suspicious falls: Knoxville, Pittsburgh, and Albany. Were there any others?" I asked after I settled on the sofa with Colonel next to me.

"Shorty and I found three more. Albuquerque, Yakima, and Boulder. The dates didn't overlap and the start and stop dates for the deaths at each location were very clear, at least to us. When Shorty's voices said the killer was close, I wiped my computer, and Shorty recorded the dates and locations. Our intention was for me to leave at the end of my contract and report our findings. Shorty told me she had a way to get the list out of the prison. When she was murdered, I panicked. I couldn't find her record and realized you were how she got the list out."

"What about Twitch?"

"Twitch is fine. She didn't know anything to tell. Her conversations don't stay on topic, and sometimes she dropped into a nonsense language that I think she makes up as she goes. Only Shorty understood her. Just to talk to her gave me a headache."

I nodded. "That's good news. I mean that she's okay. Why did you come looking for me?"

"I needed to warn you. If you have Shorty's list then you're in danger."

I furrowed my brow. "Shorty didn't give me a list. What about you? Are you in danger?"

"Yes. I don't know. Maybe. I need to find Shorty's list."

"I don't understand. Can't you just recreate the list?" Monica asked as she twirled her silver pen.

"I could with a little work. I don't remember the dates, but I'm worried the wrong person would find out about the list."

"What would be different if you recreate the list when you find the dates? Wouldn't you be in danger either way? Could Shorty have mailed her list to someone?" Monica asked. "Like a family member or her lawyer? Or given it to a visitor?"

"Not likely." Charlotte sat straighter and stiffened her back.

"Ah. But not impossible."

"I can't imagine how it could happen." Charlotte rose, clinched her fists, and paced to the back door.

"Charlotte, who do you think the killer is?" I asked in a quiet voice.

"Didn't Shorty tell you?"

"No. She never said anything about a killer or murders."

Charlotte's shoulders and hands relaxed, and a wisp of a smile disappeared when she faced me.

"We were afraid of Captain Littlefield."

I widened my eyes. "Do you have any evidence?"

"I saw him plant Duchess's bloody handkerchief." Charlotte peered at me.

My hand flew to my chest, and Monica squinted at Charlotte.

"You sure about that? You were close enough to see him?" Monica asked.

"Of course, I was." Charlotte squared off into a defensive position.

"Did you tell anyone?" Monica tapped her silver pen on the table, and her bracelets jingled.

"Of course, I didn't. I'm not a fool." Charlotte whirled and scowled at Monica. "Is that tapping necessary?"

She pushed her chair in with a hard shove. "It's obvious you don't know anything, Teach. I'll be going."

Charlotte stormed to the door and slammed it as she left.

"See why I brought her here?" Monica asked.

"If she's not the killer, she knows who is, or she's the queen of drama queens."

"I was tired of her nonsense." Monica said.

"You sure got on her nerves. I don't know if it was all the questions, the bracelets, or the silver pen. Excellent work."

"You're a star at rolling with the punches. You took it better than I expected."

I picked up Charlotte's glass and cleared the plates. "It sounds more plausible than anything we've come up with."

Monica brought her glass. "There is that. Just enough truth to make it believable."

"Sheriff told me a female serial killer didn't fit the pattern of death."

"Pattern of death. Isn't that what Shorty said she saw? So what do you think? Why did Charlotte come here?"

"To find out what I knew before she killed me. Did you catch that she'd slip between present and past tense when she talked about Twitch?"

"Now that hurt my grammar ears. She sure is easy to agitate. Her accent is not from Pittsburgh. Maybe Maryland."

I snickered. "West Virginia. I've been waiting for a chance to tell you. I found Ivy Gold in her yearbook. And Charlene Bowerton. She was a year behind Shorty."

"Charlene? Well done, Charlotte."

"I found Charlotte's current address online. The prison. Isn't that interesting?"

Monica twirled her pen, and the clink of her bracelets reminded me of a cell door closing.

"I just remembered something Shorty said when she was in my cell. *Never interrupt your enemy when she is making a mistake.*"

"Napoleon," Monica murmured, "with a slight revision. Shorty changed it to *she*."

"I need to give the sheriff's office a call."

"I'm bailing," Monica said. "Unless you think you need someone to stay with you."

I shook my head.

"See you later, Teach. Let me know what our next step is."

After she left, I called the sheriff's dispatcher, Tess, on the nonemergency line.

"Tess, tell the sheriff Charlotte is staying at the Asbury Motel. She said she came here to see if I had Shorty's list."

"You're in for it now," Tess said.

"You're right. Will I get any points for calling in before she killed me?"

Tess coughed. "Ms. Donut Lady, please don't say that to the sheriff. I have to work with him. I'll get him your message. He'll probably call right back."

"I leave around five-thirty to go to the hospital."

"He knows that. Sheriff might meet you there, but don't tell him I said that either. He's touchy lately."

Five minutes after we hung up, a car pulled in front of my house. Colonel bounded to the door, and I opened it as the sheriff stepped onto the porch.

He stormed into the house. "I thought I told you..." He closed his eyes and inhaled through his nose and out of his mouth. "She came here?"

"Charlotte contacted a realtor under the pretense of buying the computer store and is staying at the Asbury Motel. She went to the library because she heard Monica and I were friends, and they came here."

"What?"

"She told Monica she needed to meet with me in a private place."

"So now she knows where you live." The sheriff growled.

"Charlotte's been stalking me and watching the Donut Hole. She could have followed me home any time. Her goal wasn't to kill me, at least not yet. She is looking for the list. I'm certain she's convinced Shorty didn't give it to me and that I don't know anything. Maybe. She lied about where she's from and pretended Twitch was still alive. She said she left her job in a panic and claimed she was worried the list would fall into the wrong hands. I don't know what her next move might be."

I sat on the sofa, and the sheriff grabbed a kitchen chair and pulled it around to face me as he sat.

"Anything else?" he asked.

"Yes. Her name..."

My phone rang. *Asbury Motel.* I showed it to the sheriff, and he nodded as I answered and put it on speaker phone.

"Hello?"

"Hello, Teach. This is Daniel, Devlin's son. She's not feeling so good. Can you come check her? See if she needs to see the doctor? Please? You know how sick mother has been."

The sheriff nodded.

"I'll be right there."

After we hung up, I said, "Ambush."

"You sure? There's no time to plan. You can't go."

Chapter Ten

"Yes I'm sure. Daniel called me *Teach*. He calls his mother *Mama*, not mother. His call shouted *warning*. Charlotte's there; she's unstable and capable of murder. How about if I go in the front door with my phone on? You'll hear everything. It would be almost like a wire."

"Nope."

"Then Monica goes with me."

"What?"

"She's very distracting."

"Let me think."

"Sure. I'll call Monica."

Monica picked up her phone.

"What?" she asked.

"We need to go to the Asbury Motel. Shall I pick you up?"

"I'm heading back to your house. Two minutes."

I stared out the window.

"Karen. What are you thinking?"

"Shorty said, *Never interrupt your enemy when she is making a mistake.* This smells desperate. Isn't that a mistake?"

"So?"

"We don't interrupt her. We find out why she's so desperate. She may take my phone, but Monica can call you and you can listen. You'll know when it's time to intervene. If nothing else, you'll know what's happening and have the element of surprise on your side."

"No."

I shrugged. "Okay."

"You can't go. I'm arresting you."

I grabbed my phone. "I'll send Monica."

He slammed his fist on the table. "I'll arrest the entire town, if that's what it takes."

I jutted my chin. "You might want a deputy along for backup."

He frowned. "Give me five minutes to get my deputies in place. When we reach the Asbury Motel, I'm in charge. Got that?"

I rose. "Yes sir. Five minutes."

Colonel and I met Monica when she pulled into the driveway. "We've got three minutes before we can leave. I'll catch you up."

I told her about the call from Devlin's son and added, "Feel free to irritate Charlotte. I have a feeling that's our key."

Monica's eyes twinkled. "Got it."

Colonel trotted to Monica's car.

"What do you think?" I asked Monica.

She nodded. "If Colonel thinks it's a good idea then it is."

On our way to the motel, I asked, "This is crazy, isn't it? Should we have picked up bulletproof vests?"

"We're fine. Charlotte's not a shooter. She doesn't even have a gun on her."

"What? Did you check?"

"Of course, I did. I wouldn't have brought a crazed shooter into your house."

"Only a crazed killer, right?" We giggled as Monica parked. I scanned the parking lot while she called the sheriff.

"We're here. Going in."

"No cars except Charlotte's," I said.

Monica removed the phone from her pocket. "Did you hear that? Good."

I opened the car's back door, and Colonel jumped out. We hurried to the motel door, and Colonel and I led the way inside. Monica left the door open as she followed us.

Daniel stood behind the counter; his face was pale, and his mouth was pinched.

"Where is she? Have you called an ambulance?" I asked as I scanned the room.

"In the office. Not yet. Wanted your opinion first." Daniel's face brightened as he glanced at Colonel then Monica.

When I opened the office door, shadows brushed inside over my head, and I paused and ducked. Colonel barked and growled as he rushed past me. In his hurry, he bumped into me, and as I fell a whoosh of air whizzed over my head. When I went down, Daniel jumped over me, and Monica said, "Sheriff. Now."

I rose to my knees as Charlotte pulled away from Daniel's grasp. Monica stepped in front of me and waved her silver pen. When her bracelets jingled, Charlotte froze, and Monica dropped on top of me.

The sheriff shouted, "Don't move!" as he stepped past us. Colonel rumbled a low throaty growl.

Monica whispered, "We aren't."

I snorted, and she giggled as she rolled away then helped me up.

Devlin sat behind her desk, and Daniel pulled off the duct tape that had been across her mouth. "Ouch. Thanks for coming, Donut Lady, and for bringing the posse."

Two deputies rushed in and handcuffed Charlotte then led her out.

After they left, I rubbed Colonel's face. "Wish I could have thought of something biting to say when the deputies took her away. Maybe, *Excuse the interruption?*"

When Monica and I burst into laughter, Devlin joined in, and the sheriff and Daniel stared.

"See? You are the nicest friend I have," Devlin said.

I smiled. "Daniel's hints were amazing."

"I agree." The sheriff put his hand on Daniel's shoulder. "Have you thought about law enforcement? If you're interested, I know of a scholarship." Daniel beamed.

"By the way, Karen, you are fired," the sheriff glowered.

Monica took my arm. "We're leaving before you get to the guilty-by-association part, Sheriff."

We strolled to her car, and Colonel trotted by my side.

On the way to my house, I said, "Finally. Now I can put all my focus on Woody."

"Ms. Karen, time to leave." Woody's nurse had placed her hand on my arm to wake me. "You need to get some rest yourself. You've been here every day all week." She picked up the graphic novel that had fallen to the floor and handed it to me. "We've noticed he isn't as restless when you're reading to him. He's getting better. You'll see."

I was sure his eyelids flickered. "Hi, Woody. We miss you at the shop. Colonel and Mia would visit you if the hospital allowed animals. You get better. We'll wait for you."

The next day, Woody opened his eyes while I read. "Donut."

I laughed and brushed away a pesky tear. "If you want a donut, I'll smuggle one in for you, Woody."

The corners of his mouth lifted in a weak smile.

His nurse tapped on the door. "Woody needs his rest."

"Donut, Miss," Woody said in a stronger voice.

The nurse's eyes widened. "Woody, if you want a donut, I'm sure Miss will find a way to bring you one."

After I cleaned the equipment and shop the next morning, I hurried to the hospital with a donut wrapped in a napkin for Woody. The hospital staff joined in the smuggled donut game and turned away to hide their grins.

I tapped on the door. "You alone?" I asked. "I've got a chocolate donut for you."

Woody sat up straighter in his bed. "Donuts make me better."

I handed him his pastry and settled in the chair next to his bed. I held our book to my chest. "Can I ask a couple of questions?"

Woody had stuffed half the donut into his mouth. He nodded.

I smiled. "We're not in a rush, so finish chewing before you answer but why did you stay in the shed?"

Woody chewed and swallowed then gulped down the milk that was on his tray. "The man got mad. He said I ate more than what the county paid for and other stuff. I hid in the shed where he couldn't see me."

"That's logical. What about the bananas? Was that an extra snack for you?"

"No Miss Lady. The little girl was hungry, and she loved bananas better than anything except donuts." He hung his head. "I stole a donut every day for her."

"That's not stealing. Remember I told you no limit? That included donuts. That's sharing and being kind to someone who needs help. We take donuts to the soup kitchen to share and be kind. It was smart of you to think of giving her a donut. Nobody else could have done it but you."

He mumbled, "I was afraid you'd find out and not let me come to the shop anymore. I forgot about the soup kitchen."

"You okay now?" I asked.

"Yes Miss." He gazed at me, and I smiled at the warmth and trust in his eyes.

"Good. Let's read."

He settled back on his pillow. "Let's read."

Later that week, I heard a tap on the shop door while I was dropping sprinkles on the French vanilla glaze donuts. The sheriff stood at the door. In place of his usual smile, his mouth was set, and his eyes narrowed. I couldn't read his face, and I had a bad feeling in my stomach.

I unlocked the door, and the sheriff strode in. I reached for the coffee pot and filled two cups.

"Ms. Karen, we need to talk. Something's been bothering me for a while. I woke up again early this morning thinking about it. It's none of my business from an official standpoint, but as a friend, I can't seem to let it go."

I sat next to him at the counter and set down the cups.

His face softened, and he sipped his hot coffee. "You are the nicest person I know. Do you mind telling me what led up to your manslaughter charge?"

I glanced at the window. A trick in the street lights reflected an illusion of my twenty-five-year-old face. She smiled, and I returned her smile.

"We can do this," she said. I nodded and turned to face the sheriff.

"I met my husband in college. We were married the week after we graduated. He had numerous affairs, but he'd beg me to forgive him, and I would. But then about fifteen years ago, I discovered his latest girlfriend had a pre-teen daughter, and Terry... he abused her. Physically. Sexually."

The sheriff slammed his hand on the counter. The sound and force of the impact startled me. His face was a volcano ready to explode. The shadows gathered near the front window.

"Why didn't you divorce him? Turn him in?"

I hung my head in the shame I'd carried all these years. "He was very manipulative. He convinced me our failed marriage was my fault. I learned about the young girl because he told me. Bragged."

I pressed my hand to my ear because I still heard his disgusting words inside my head.

"I was shocked; I didn't want to believe anyone could be so vile. I pushed Terry away. We were on the front porch, and he was near the steps. He lost his balance, fell, and broke his arm when he went down. He was a high school football player with a solid build, and even though he'd let himself go and was out of shape, I was amazed I'd pushed him hard enough to make him lose his balance. He laughed and called the police. He told them I broke his arm and added I didn't mean to hurt him. He insisted I always apologized afterward, and I was arrested. He refused x-rays. Said he'd see his own doctor. It was a nightmare." I shuddered.

Sheriff Grady cleared his throat. "No x-rays, huh?"

I shook my head. "You need a donut?"

He shifted in his seat and grinned. "Is that a trick question? I'm kinda partial to sprinkles."

I grabbed two plates. Sprinkles for him; maple for me.

"I told the police about the girl, and they talked to the girlfriend. She denied any abuse of her daughter. No one talked to the little girl. After that, Terry injured himself and claimed I was responsible. He took large doses of aspirin in front of me so I would know why he bruised so easily. He'd go to the doctor or emergency room and tell them I did it, and he'd always add in his faked unconvincing way that I didn't mean it. Of course, they were obligated to call the police. He assumed the persona of a victim and portrayed me as a violent person."

"This is hard to listen to." The sheriff shook his head. "I can't imagine how hard it was to live through it."

"It was horrible. The house was in my name, and I paid all the bills, but I moved out and filed for divorce. I met with the girlfriend and learned he blackmailed her. He told her he'd prove she prostituted her daughter, and he'd get custody of the girl. She told me she knew intellectually there was no way he'd get custody of her daughter, but if anybody could figure out a way to get custody, Terry could. I agreed with her. He was slimy. She said she was terrified of him and what he might do next. I understood."

Sheriff gazed into his empty cup. I smiled at his look of longing.

Subtle.

I poured refills and took a sip. "I returned to my house to pick up a few things. He was supposed to be out of town, but after I backed out of the driveway to leave, he stepped into the street in front of me. I stopped, and he taunted me, said terrible, graphic things about the little girl. He turned to walk away, and I stomped on the gas."

I wiped my sweaty hands on my apron. The urge to flee still lingered. "I wanted to get away from him as fast as I could. He whirled back around and stepped in front of my car. I think he meant for me to graze him, but he misjudged the distance."

The sheriff narrowed his eyes. "There's more."

Wisps of shadows drifted inside under the front door.

"I lifted my foot to brake, but..." I bit my lip.

Colonel nudged my hand with his nose, and I scratched his ear.

"I'll never know for sure if it was intentional or panic, but my foot slammed the accelerator. Sometimes I've hoped it was intentional. At the split second before the impact, he grinned at me through the windshield. Like he knew he would be badly injured or die, and he was happy because I'd be blamed." I shuddered.

I could still see Terry's face. I closed my eyes, but the wicked grin stayed.

Sheriff Grady and I sat in silence.

I cleared my throat. "I've never told anyone the entire story. I'm not even sure I'd ever put all the pieces together in my head."

The shadows swirled and danced.

Grady shook his head. I saw sorrow on his face. "I knew there had to be something. Something more. I didn't know how bad it was."

"I was in shock, and I felt like whatever happened to me after that was worth it. Terry was gone, and the little girl was safe. I found the records Terry created to prove he was the girl's biological father and discovered how to release his life insurance money to the girlfriend based on his claims. It was a sizeable sum, and she could afford a good school for her daughter and counseling for both of them."

"You need a good lawyer to help sort all this out. I'll do whatever I can to help you," Grady said.

"I guess you're right. I will just as soon as Woody's well now that Charlotte's caught."

———ele———

After we closed the shop, Colonel walked with me to the hospital. He waited outside the sliding doors and greeted staff and visitors.

I stopped by the nurses' station for a report. The charge nurse walked with me to the elevator. "Woody's growing stronger." She smiled as I pushed the elevator button. "We're positive it's the magic pink sprinkles."

———ele———

Three days later, I sat next to Woody's bed and watched him eat his daily donut.

"Get into any trouble today?" he asked.

I sighed. "I might have topped Geoff."

"Good one, Miss. Tell me about it?"

I walked to the window and gazed at the clear blue sky with high, fluffy clouds. "Yes."

I scooted the visitor's chair closer to his bed. "It's kind of a hard story to tell. The story started a long time ago. I was married to a man who wasn't very nice."

I told Woody about Terry and being in prison. "Then after I moved back, I bought the donut shop. You know the rest." I held my breath and waited.

Woody frowned. "What does the sheriff say?"

I didn't expect that.

"The sheriff says I need a good lawyer."

"Then we need to find you a good lawyer. I'll go to law school, but we don't want to wait that long, do we?"

I chuckled. "You will be a great lawyer."

I walked to his door. *Where's that nurse to kick me out?*

I cleared my throat. "There's a little more. I can't be a foster parent."

Woody's eyes widened. "Are you sure, Miss?"

"I'm positive."

"So what do we do?" Woody's breathing quickened, his machines beeped, and alarms squealed. I hurried back to his bedside and took his hand.

"We find you a good foster parent. Your caseworker assured me she had a good temporary home for you until they find a foster parent. One we'd approve of. We've got her attention. We'll be fine."

He looked at me. "We'll be fine?" The beeps on his machines slowed. The alarms quieted.

I nodded. "Yes we will."

He leaned back, and the beeps silenced as his face relaxed. "Then we find a good lawyer."

The next afternoon, I read the first part of a book and held the book while Woody read to me until his eyes drooped and his head nodded. I marked our place for the next day with a bookmark one of Woody's classmates made for him. Woody leaned back, stared at the ceiling, and frowned.

"Something bothering you?" I asked.

"I been worried about the little girl. She was hungry. She'd sneak into the shed at night, and I'd give her food. I wanted to take her when I ran away, but she was locked in her room. Is she okay? Is somebody feeding her?"

"She's okay." My eyes welled up, and I cleared my throat. "She's with her family now, and they make sure she's fed, warm, and happy."

Woody turned to me and smiled then closed his eyes. "That's good."

"Yes," I whispered. "Yes it is."

After I left the hospital, I went to the school and met with the principal and his teacher. I read them the riot act, in a nice way, about Woody not knowing how to read.

Early the next morning his teacher came into the shop with a typed list in her hand. "I've developed a plan for Haywood to catch up with his age group. Let me know if you have any questions. And thank you for being such a strong advocate for this boy who somehow fell through the cracks. I'm very sorry about that."

I sent her to school with four dozen donuts for his class from Woody.

Four days later, I waited for the elevator to take me down to the lobby. I gazed at the floor. The whirs and dings of the elevator mimicked my rambling thoughts.

A man cleared his throat, and I glanced up. The sheriff smiled. "I was on my way to see you. We have a foster parent for Woody. She was approved today. She said you and Woody have to approve too before she accepts, and if the two of you are interested, he can continue to help you and study at the Donut Hole."

"Who? Is it someone we know?" My mind raced. *Giselle? A nurse? Monica?*

"Well, yes. She wanted to wait for you at the Donut Hole. She wants to tell you herself. Want a ride?"

Colonel was waiting for us when we left the hospital. The sheriff opened the passenger's door on his car for me and the back door for Colonel. Colonel jumped in like he belonged there.

"Colonel looks awfully comfortable in the back of the squad car," the sheriff said.

"Like a boss," I added.

The drive to the shop took forever. "You missed a turn again, Sheriff. I could have walked in half the time it's taking you to drive to the shop." I grumbled. Colonel whined. "See, even my back-up agrees."

The sheriff grinned. "Safety first."

SWEET DEAL SEALED

I was ready to scream "Just go!" by the time we pulled up.

Shirley stood at the shop door. I exhaled in a fit of deflation and slumped in my seat.

"Why is she here? I don't have any fresh donuts." I tried not to sound peevish, but I think I failed.

When the car stopped, Shirley jerked open the passenger's door and dragged me out. "I did it. I'm a foster mother, and Woody can live with me if it's okay with you and with him. I got help, Karen, so I can come into your shop again. My counselor said she'd give me a note. It's in my purse." She reached into her purse and pulled out an envelope addressed to *The Donut Lady*.

My mouth dropped open.

"Take it! Will you go with me to see Woody? Would you introduce us and tell him I'm a nice person?" Shirley asked.

I took the envelope and nodded. Grady grinned.

"Good. It's a deal," Shirley said.

I hugged her. "Deal sealed, Shirley."

"Can we go to the hospital now? Will you ride with me? You don't mind riding with me, do you? I'll be nice," Shirley said.

I rode with Shirley to the hospital.

"I can't really cook," she said on the way. "The county extension agent said I could take lessons, and she helped me draw up a menu plan to use when Haywood gets out of the hospital. I forgot to ask anyone if Haywood has any food allergies. Do you think I should get a dog? And a cat? Is it okay if I call him Woody? Does he play baseball? I was a pretty good softball pitcher. Remember how much

I love to play? I loved my red uniform. I could help him. I mean when he gets stronger. I don't know anything about soccer. Do you think he'd rather play soccer? I asked the extension agent if I could take a class on what boys like to do, and she helped me sign up for a single-parent support class."

I smiled. *Shirley hasn't mellowed a bit.*

Shirley took a quick breath and continued her monologue on our way into the hospital, up the elevator, and down the hallway. I'd quit listening before we reached the hospital parking lot.

I felt a tug on my shirt sleeve. "Karen. Karen. Where's Haywood's room? We're at the end of the hallway."

"Sorry. I was. Distracted." Lame, but it was the best I could come up with on short notice.

I turned around and led the way to Woody's room. When I stepped inside, I smiled at Woody then realized Shirley hadn't come in with me. She lingered in the hallway. I grabbed her arm and pulled her inside.

"Shirley, this is Woody. Woody, this is Ms. Shirley. She's been my friend for a long time, and she's a nice person. She'd like to be your foster mother."

The room was quiet. Woody squinted at Shirley with his interrogator gaze. Shirley froze like she was a frail antelope, and he was a lion ready to pounce.

After a long silence, Woody said, "Get in any trouble today?"

I put my hand over my mouth. Shirley's eyes widened. "Yes, but I apologized. Is that okay?"

"Yes, ma'am, Ms. Shirley, but I need to read you a story about Geoff."

I couldn't hold back the chuckle. "You two will be just fine."

———*ele*———

Later that afternoon, I hid in my sanctuary, the pink room, with my phone in my lap and Colonel on the floor next to me. Mia stalked shadows in the corner. I had the still-folded list of lawyers from John Padilla in my hand. "I don't know if I'm ready to open an old wound, Colonel."

Colonel rolled onto his back and fell asleep with his paws in the air. Mia stalked Colonel.

I stared at the paper and shuddered as Terry's hate-filled words bombarded me. A sharp knock at the door startled me.

"Closed. I'm closed." My shout woke Colonel, and he padded out of the pink room to investigate the sound.

The persistent knocking echoed throughout the shop, and Colonel whined. When I reached the pink room door, Monica twirled her silver pen and opened the front door.

"You were too slow." She grinned and locked the door behind her. "Were you in your office? Have any leftover donuts?"

I stared at her. "I was in the pink room. Is this a donut emergency? I don't have any."

"Had to ask." She shrugged. "I brought brownies. Pink room is perfect. Let's sit." Monica breezed past me and sat at the table. She raised her eyebrows, and I sat next to her.

"This is an emergency. I couldn't have waited one more minute." She handed me a brownie then munched on hers.

After she swallowed, she said, "Do you want the long version or the short version?"

"What?" I asked with my mouth full.

"Thought so. One of my new librarian friends who helped me search for Charlotte in the system sent me a link then called me to give me more details. I sent the link to your email so you can read it later. That's the long version. Here's the short version. Charlotte was at the courthouse for arraignment. The courtroom was on the third floor, and the elevator was out of order. She and two guards were climbing the open stairwell and were near the third floor when Charlotte screamed, "No! Poison Ivy!" then tumbled over the railing and fell to the marble lobby. Dead, of course. The official report is she lost her balance and fell. My friend, however, said the original report was that she had been tossed over the railing." Monica finished her brownie. "Delicious."

She leaned back in her chair and smiled. "I love donuts, brownies, and justice."

"Do you think Shorty pushed her over?" My eyes widened. "Or do you think Charlotte saw Shorty and lost her balance trying to get away?"

"I don't care." Monica cackled and headed to the front door.

I smiled as I locked the door after she left. *Maybe I can make that call after all.*

When I returned to the pink room and unfolded the paper, my eyes widened. I picked up my phone and tapped in the number for the first lawyer John recommended.

"Hello, Amber? I need a good lawyer, and I understand you're the best."

Are you ready for the next Donut Lady book?
SWEET DEAL CONCEALED, Book 2
Donut Lady is threatened by a violent man. After he is murdered, the killer stalks her. Donut Lady is the next to die.

Donut Lady's terror of nightmares and shadows from her years in prison haunts her. After a violent man who threatened Karen is murdered, her nightmares foretell of a tragic, second murder.

The killer stalks the Donut Lady; she does not intend to become victim number three, but can the Donut Lady and her shadows expose what the murderer has concealed for years? She's fierce, but the killer's scheme is to watch her die.

Find SWEET DEAL CONCEALED at Barrett Book Shop BarrettBookShop.com

An independent online Book Shop owned by the author, Judith A. Barrett

Did you enjoy Donut Lady's story?

Leave a review or a rating (reviews are helpful for other readers; retailers rank books by ratings) with Barrett Book Shop or your favorite book retailer!

You keep reading; I'll keep writing!

Let's stay in touch!
SUBSCRIBE to Judith's newsletter for stories, exclusive bargains, and news of the next book!
judithabarrett.com/newsletter

About the Author

Judith's motto: *You keep reading; I'll keep writing!* Judith A. Barrett, award-winning author, lives on a farm in Georgia with her husband, two dogs, and chickens. She writes series for her readers: cozy mystery, romantic mystery, thriller, and survival, post-apoc novels with unusual sidekicks.

When she isn't writing, Judith is busy working on the farm, camping with her husband and dogs (but still writing), or relaxing on her front porch while she watches the beautiful sunset and wonders what the characters are plotting next in her current book.

Check out her Website at judithabarrett.com
Subscribe to her newsletter on her website:
judithabarrett.com/newsletter
Her online Book Store is BarrettBookshop.com
Buy your next ebook, audio book, or signed paperback directly from the author!